P. D.

Pups tha

Therapy dogs work their magic this Christmas!

Welcome to Christmas at Heatherglen Clinic!

Set in a beautiful castle, nestled in the Highlands of Scotland, it's the perfect place for patients to recover and rehabilitate from their injuries.

The medical professionals working at this exclusive estate are dedicated to mending their patients, but the magic of this special place and the clinic's adorable four-legged therapy partners help heal even the most broken of hearts and bring happily-ever-afters to both staff and patients alike!

Discover how healing pups help make Christmas miracles happen in this brand-new miniseries guaranteed to leave paw prints on your heart!

Highland Doc's Christmas Rescue by Susan Carlisle

Festive Fling with the Single Dad by Annie Claydon

Making Christmas Special Again by Annie O'Neil

Their One-Night Christmas Gift by Karin Baine

Available now!

Dear Reader,

I'm so privileged to work with these other lovely authors again in creating a whole new world for you to dive into. When the idea of a series based around PAT dogs at Christmas was discussed, we knew exactly where we wanted to base it. Scotland!

It's been so much fun researching for this one and I may have taken one or two trips across the water to get that authentic feel…

Charles, my brooding neurologist, has everything he ever wanted in his beautiful castle and bustling clinic. Except for the woman he loved. Staying loyal to the memories of his brother and father came at a heavy price. He let Harriet go to save her from the burden of Heatherglen Castle, but now she's back. One steamy night together has brought them to another crossroads and this time they both have to make the decision whether to stay or go.

I hope you enjoy this series and it gives you that warm Christmassy glow when you're reading it.

Have a happy New Year!

Love,

Karin xx

THEIR ONE-NIGHT CHRISTMAS GIFT

KARIN BAINE

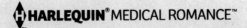

Recycling programs
for this product may
not exist in your area.

ISBN-13: 978-1-335-64196-0

Their One-Night Christmas Gift

First North American Publication 2019

Copyright © 2019 by Karin Baine

Printed in U.S.A.

HARLEQUIN®
www.Harlequin.com

Books by Karin Baine

Harlequin Medical Romance

Single Dad Docs
The Single Dad's Proposal
Paddington Children's Hospital
Falling for the Foster Mom

French Fling to Forever
A Kiss to Change Her Life
The Doctor's Forbidden Fling
The Courage to Love Her Army Doc
Reforming the Playboy
Their Mistletoe Baby
From Fling to Wedding Ring
Midwife Under the Mistletoe
Their One-Night Twin Surprise

Visit the Author Profile page
at Harlequin.com for more titles.

For Richard Rankin xx

**Praise for
Karin Baine**

"Karin Baine is a brilliant writer. She takes you on a journey as the characters develop and find their inner strength and happiness. I recommend her books to any romance lover!"

CHAPTER ONE

CHARLES ROSS-WYLDE WAS a selfish, cold-hearted liar and Harriet Bell was better off without him. At least, that was what she'd spent the last twelve years telling herself.

The reality of seeing him again was very different from the scenario she'd imagined. She'd been shocked to see him here, but so far she'd resisted slapping him, throwing a drink in his face, or announcing to the rest of the conference attendees that *he* was the reason she couldn't risk loving anyone again. Perhaps she'd matured or, more likely, hadn't expected to feel anything other than pure hatred towards him.

She watched him now from the other side of the room as the assembled medical community enjoyed the tea break between lectures. It gave her time to study him un-

noticed and decide what she wanted to do—
if anything. If she chose to she could walk
out of here and he'd be none the wiser, with
nothing changing their current status quo.

Impossible when there was so much she
wanted to say, so much she wanted him to
explain.

Physically, he hadn't changed much from
the man who'd once promised her their lives
would be spent together except he looked
older...more manly.

He was still trying to sweep that floppy
dark hair back into a neat style befitting a
professional man, though she remembered
all too well how it had looked first thing in
the morning tousled by sleep. And, as always, he was dressed impeccably, the navy
suit tailored to his exact measurements. The
beard was new, the dark shadow along his
jawline making him look even more mascu-
line, if that was possible. It suited him—as
did the glasses he was sporting.

Damn it, he was still gorgeous, and apparently still able to make her heart flutter ma-
niacally as though she'd just run a marathon.

'They really should have an open bar,' she

muttered to the bewildered woman serving refreshments to the masses, turning away from the view of her ex-fiancé and wishing for a tot of whisky in her coffee.

Not that she drank often, but she'd make an exception to help her escape memories of her and Charles—good and bad. She'd have to make do with an extra spoonful of sugar in her tea to help with the shock.

'I didn't expect to see you here.' That soft, Scottish burr capable of rendering her into a gibbering wreck tickled the back of her neck. He'd found her.

Harriet fumbled with her cup and saucer, spilling the contents over herself right before she turned around to face him. 'Charles. What a surprise.'

'Sorry, I didn't mean to startle you.' He grabbed a napkin from the buffet table and started dabbing at the stain darkening the front of her dress.

'I can do that, thanks.' She didn't mean to snap but she couldn't bear to have him touch her after all this time when she didn't know what emotions it would unleash.

'Sorry.' He handed over possession of the

napkin so she could tend to the ruined dress herself. 'It was just nice to see a familiar face. How have you been, Harriet?'

There was no sign of remorse for the relationship and future he'd thrown away. He was talking to her as though they were old school friends, who had no real emotional connection and had simply happened to run into each other.

She set the wet napkin and coffee back on the table and took a moment to consider her response. If she kicked off and made a scene it would be clear she'd never got over him and that would most likely send Charles running. She didn't know what she wanted from him, but it wasn't that.

'Oh, you know, keeping busy. You?' She plastered on a smile, willing to play along with this game until one of them broke. Her, probably.

'The same. I took up a placement in Glasgow to complete my medical training and set up a clinic at Heatherglen. It was initially to help army veterans, but we've extended to provide state-of-the-art medical facilities for physical and emotional rehabilitation to a wider range of patients.'

'Sounds impressive.' Inheriting his father's fortune and the family estate had signalled the end of their engagement so it was difficult for Harriet to be as enthusiastic about his accomplishments as she should have been.

'I wanted to do something worthwhile to honour my brother and father, but it takes a lot of upkeep. I don't get to make as many trips to London as I'd like.' His older brother, Nick, had served with the military in Afghanistan. Unfortunately, he'd been killed by a roadside bomb before Harriet had had the chance to meet him. That family tragedy, followed by the death of his father about a year later, had proved too much for Charles and their wedding plans.

'I'm the same, too many responsibilities here to even take a holiday these days.' Needless to say, she hadn't been back to Scotland since his father's funeral, when Charles had gone back on his promise of making a life with her. At the time she'd believed grief had driven his decision, but when he'd failed to follow her back to London she'd soon realised he was serious about no longer wanting to marry her. It was difficult to reconcile that man who'd broken her heart with the one stood before her now, making small talk.

'So, you did stay here after all? I'd hoped you would.' He was smiling so Harriet didn't think he was trying to rub salt into the wound he'd inflicted on her that day. She'd never received a proper explanation as to why he'd called things off. Goodness knew, she'd been desperate for one, but she'd eventually had to accept the simple truth that he didn't want her any more. She'd seen that happen between her own parents when she'd been young and had watched her mother torture herself trying to figure out what she'd done wrong when her father had walked out on them. There was no way she was spending the rest of her life beating herself up about it, the way her mother had until her death.

'Yes. I'm an orthopaedic surgeon.'

Top of my field, she wanted to add, piqued by the fact he'd never bothered to check up and see what she'd been doing. Then again, she hadn't done that either, afraid she'd start obsessing over him or what could have been between them. In his case it seemed it was merely down to a lack of interest.

'Neurologist,' he countered. 'I thought it made sense to take that path, so I'd be able to better treat veterans.'

What a team they would have made working together but perhaps she wouldn't have pursued her career so doggedly if they had married. When she and Charles had been together she'd imagined she could have it all—a career and a family. She'd thought they were a team, on an equal footing and willing to share the responsibilities of raising children. Except the moment Charles's circumstances had changed he'd backed out and left her to pick up the pieces of her broken heart. She'd paid the price for his actions.

Perhaps she'd had a lucky escape. If he'd proved so unreliable further down the line, he could have left her raising their children alone once he'd decided he didn't want her after all. As it was, she'd poured her heart and soul into her career because that was the one thing she could count on always being there. Things happened for a reason and she had no regrets when it had moved her focus back onto her work. It didn't look as though he had any either.

They fell into an awkward gap in conversation, neither apparently knowing what to say to the other but not wanting to make the first move in walking away.

'Could all attendees please make their way back to their seats for the next talk, please?'

The announcement over the loudspeaker filled the silence on their behalf and left them with the decision of whether to say goodbye temporarily, or for ever.

'Listen, why don't we go for a proper drink? The hotel bar should be quiet enough with all the reprobates locked in here for another few hours of telling us things we already know.' Charles rested his hand lightly at her waist, leaning in so his comment reached only her ears. She could barely feel the pressure of his fingertips on her skin, but it was sufficient to awaken every erogenous zone in her body until she was sure she'd follow him to the ends of the earth.

'Sure,' she squeaked.

Damn, she was in trouble.

Charles didn't know what he hoped to gain by getting Harriet on her own, except having her to himself for the first time in over a decade. When he'd spotted her across the room there had been no great plan, just a need to be near her. Much like the first time they'd met in medical school and had instantly become inseparable. Being each other's first loves, they'd become serious quickly. In hindsight, that youth and inexperience would never have worked in a world where tradition and duty to the family name was everything. He'd just wanted to be with Harriet and had given no thought to Heatherglen back then.

Now he considered himself lucky she'd agreed to go for a drink with him instead of throwing a cup of hot coffee in his face.

'There's a seat in the corner. I'll get the drinks. White wine?' He led her into the bar, where one or two other hotel guests had sought refuge.

'Yes, please.' Even that knowledge of her preferred drink brought back memories of times together it was difficult to ignore. Those early student days of being silly and partying too hard. Later, when it had been a bottle of wine to accompany a romantic meal they often hadn't bothered to finish...

'Charles, what are you doing?' he muttered under his breath, and stole a glance back at Harriet as she settled into the corner.

Those days of acting only in his own interests were supposed to be far behind him. He didn't make any decisions now without thinking through how it might affect those around him. It had been a tough lesson to learn when the consequences of his past actions had come at the price of his brother and father's lives. He'd sacrificed his relationship with Harriet for her benefit—his first act of selflessness when he'd inherited Heatherglen. Not that she'd known, and he couldn't have told her it was because he'd wanted her to stay on in London and pursue her career instead of getting dragged into his mess. She would've insisted on going to Scotland with him.

Although, seeing her now and realising everything he'd lost, regret weighed heavily on his shoulders along with his threefold burden of guilt.

Approaching her this evening and getting her to agree to join him for a drink had been entirely for his own benefit without considering her feelings. Yet, so far, she'd shown him nothing but friendliness in return. It was entirely possible he'd over-inflated the idea of what they'd had together in his head and she'd forgotten him the second she'd got on that train without him.

'You look good, by the way. Have I said that already?' He'd certainly thought it as he'd headed back to her.

Harriet had always been pretty with her slim figure and long, dark blonde hair but now she was a stunningly beautiful woman. The emerald-green dress she was wearing wasn't particularly noteworthy except for the womanly figure it clung to, accentuating her every curve. It was understated and sophisticated, but on Harriet it was as sexy as hell.

'You haven't but thank you.' She sipped her wine, leaving a trace of ruby lip gloss on the rim of her glass, and...he really needed to keep his libido in check. She was his ex-fiancée, not an anonymous one-night stand.

'So, are you married? Any kids?' He took a gulp of lager, making the question as non-chalant as he could. Why should it matter to him what her marital status was, other than cooling his jets if he found out there was someone waiting for her at home?

'No. I decided my career was the only long-term relationship I needed in my life. I'm too busy to fall for all that again.'

Ouch.

Harriet's brown eyes glittered with a dark challenge for him to bite back. Charles didn't want to go down that route, going over old ground and spoiling the moment they were having now, but she deserved some sort of explanation.

'What about you? Did you settle down?'

'I'm too busy with the clinic and, to be honest, Mum isn't the best advert for marriage. I'm not sure what number husband she's on now since Dad. Three, I think. She spends her days sailing around in his supery-acht. We don't see very much of her. I think Heatherglen holds too many sad memories for her.'

'I know the feeling.' Harriet took another sip of her wine, apparently needing to dull the mention of his family home with alcohol.

'Harriet, about all that...' There had to be some way of saying 'It wasn't you, it was me', without sounding completely insincere.

She saved him the trouble, reaching out her hand to still his, which was currently ripping up the cardboard beer mat. 'This is much too serious a topic for this evening, Charles.'

Suddenly his mind was spinning, trying to come to terms with the way his body was responding to her touch after all this time apart and to what she was saying to him.

'I don't do serious any more.' She held him with her ever-darkening gaze, making no attempt to break contact.

'No? What *do* you do?' He leaned in closer, hoping that if she was actually coming on to him, it wasn't simply a ploy to get revenge.

'I have fun, Charles. You do remember how to do that, don't you? If so, I'm in Room 429.' With that, she got up and walked away. Leaving Charles with his mouth open, his heart hammering, and battling with his conscience, which was telling him that following her was a really bad idea.

Harriet's legs shook on her way towards the elevator. She'd never been so brazen in her life and couldn't even blame it on the alcohol when she'd only had a sip. From the moment she'd seen Charles, she'd wanted what they'd had in the past. Wanted him. What she didn't want was to rake over the ashes of the past and be reminded of how he'd rejected her. It was important to know he was still attracted to her. As though that would somehow erase the previous damage he'd caused her self-esteem.

One night with her ex, on her terms, might give her closure on the relationship that had spoiled her for any other.

Except he hadn't immediately jumped up and begged to take her there and then. She'd merely succeeded in humiliating herself and now had an extra chapter to add to their tragic story.

She jabbed and jabbed at the button for the lift, wishing it would somehow make it come faster. Then it would swallow her up and transport her away from view as soon as possible.

'Harriet, wait!' Charles shouted after her as she stepped inside the lift. It was tempting to let the doors shut in his face and be done with him once and for all, but he jammed his foot inside and stole that option from her.

The only scenario worse than being stood up when you'd offered yourself on a plate to a man was having him tell you why he didn't want to sleep with you. She fought off the tears already blurring her vision because she was determined not to re-create their last mortifying goodbye.

'Are you sure you want to do this?' His brow was furrowed, and she could see he was actually contemplating her proposal, not attempting to let her down easily at all.

That reassurance buoyed her spirits once more, along with her intention to seduce him. 'It's not a big deal, Charles. We're both single, hard-working professionals who want to let off a little steam in a hotel room.'

Now that she knew she had his interest, she stepped so close to him they were toe to toe.

'We both know it would be more than that.' There was a thread of resistance left in his words, yet his eyes and body were saying something different.

They'd spent enough time together for her to know when he was aroused, and vice versa.

'It doesn't have to be.' She didn't have to fake anything to convince him she wanted this no-strings fling when her breathy voice was a natural reaction to having him so close again.

'I know I hurt you, Harriet. Sleeping together now isn't going to change that. It isn't going to change anything. I'm still going to go back to Heatherglen and your life is here.' He was pointing out the obvious to her, they weren't getting back together no matter what happened tonight. It wasn't an outright rejection, though, because he was reaching out to her, caressing her cheek with his thumb, letting her know this was her decision. She was all right with that, safe in the knowledge she was in control of what happened next.

'I'm not looking to rekindle a romance. The past is done with but it's clear that the chemistry is still there between us.' She stroked a finger down the front of his shirt, revelling in the desire darkening his eyes until they were almost black. This was what she wanted—confirmation that she still affected him as much as he did her. More importantly, she needed this to give her some closure.

She'd used Charles as an excuse not to let anyone else get close to her but recently she'd begun to wonder if she was missing something in her life. If she was ever to entertain the notion of a serious relationship, or even a family, she had to put Charles's memory to rest first. One more time together and a chance to say a proper goodbye should finally close that chapter of her life.

'As I remember, that was never a problem for us, but we do have a long, complicated history. Is it really a good idea to go back there?'

'Now isn't the time to start getting chivalrous, Charles.' Harriet let her finger trail down until she reached his belt buckle, then started to undo it.

Charles let out a groan. 'I just don't want us to do anything that will end up with you getting hurt again. I can't give you any more now than I could all those years ago.'

'All I'm asking for is tonight. I'm not going to beg.' She popped open the button on his trousers then stopped. If he wanted more he was going to have to say so.

'One night?'

'We never got to say goodbye. Let's think of it as us both getting closure.'

'Going out with a bang?' he asked with a smirk, but he was close enough she could hear the hitch in his breathing. Clearly, he wasn't as composed as he was making out.

'Something like that. A one-time offer never to be repeated or spoken of again.'

'Deal.' His voice was a growl as he wound his arm around her waist, pulled her tight to his body and covered her lips with his.

Just like that the touch paper was lit, their passion reignited in an instant. The kiss so urgent and demanding it took her breath away. She didn't remember Charles being quite so…masterful. Perhaps it was that knowledge they were being reckless that added an extra frisson to their passion. This was definitely the last time they'd be together and would be a sweeter memory, she hoped, to hold onto than the last one.

He backed her against the wall of the lift, his mouth, his tongue never leaving hers. Arousal swept through her, showing no mercy or regard for their location or history. Harriet felt along the wall for the control panel and hit the button for the fourth floor. Charles paused their amorous reunion to hit the one for the second floor instead.

'My room's closer,' he whispered against her neck, and she felt the effect of his warm breath on her skin all the way down to her toes.

The thing about being her past lover was that he remembered exactly where to strike to make her weak at the knees. He knew all her sensitive spots and she shivered with anticipation at the thought of him using that advantage. Two could play that game and it wasn't long before they were both gasping with pleasure as they began to reacquaint themselves with each other. If either of them had booked the penthouse suite she doubted whether they would've made it out of here without consummating their renewed acquaintance.

The doors opened, and they were soon fumbling their way down the corridor, steadfastly locked in their passionate embrace. Charles smiled against her lips as he tried to unlock the room door behind her. They were giggling young lovers again, driven by their hormones and lust, and Harriet was ignoring her adult brain telling her otherwise.

'Have you got any protection?' As they fell through the door her mind was racing ahead. She didn't want to interrupt a crucial moment to track down some condoms in case it gave either of them time to think about what they were doing and change their mind.

'Somewhere.'

He backed her over to the large bed, raining kisses along her neck and collarbone until she fell onto the mattress in a puddle of ecstasy. With one hand he fished in his pocket for his wallet and produced a foil packet. Harriet was glad he didn't have a drawer full of condoms by the bed stocked up for a weekend of bedroom antics with faceless women. A hook-up had come as much of a surprise to him as it had to her but now it was happening she was glad one of them had come prepared.

She helped him shed his jacket and set to work unbuttoning his shirt, longing for the feel of his skin beneath her fingertips. Finding that patch of hair on his chest reminded her how familiar his body was to her but, oh, how she wanted to get to know it intimately again. Her hands at his fly, she began to undo his trousers.

'Harriet? I want to make this last,' he gasped as she pulled him free from the constraints of his clothes.

'I want you. Now,' she demanded. This had to be on her terms, so she remained in control. The only way she could justify bedding her ex was to treat him as casually as he had her. She had needs and though she'd taken lovers since Charles, only he could give her what she truly wanted.

Charles didn't protest. Instead, he slid his hand beneath her dress and tugged her underwear away. With their clothes half on, half off, and Harriet's dress hitched up around her waist, she waited with bated breath for him to sheath himself. There was something daring and incredibly sexy about the spontaneity of it all. She was risking everything she had by bedding him one more time when he'd had the power in the past to topple her world around her.

'I guess we do have all night to get to know each other again.' Charles smiled at her in the darkness and Harriet arched to meet him at their most sensitive parts. She wanted their bodies to do all the talking tonight. That way there could be no confusion about what she expected from him. This was only about sex. An area she knew he excelled in.

They clung to one another, perspiration settling on their skins as they raced towards that moment of utter bliss they knew they could find with each other. Harriet was already on her way to hitting that peak as though she'd been waiting for twelve long years to do this with him again. Those years apart certainly hadn't diminished their appetites for one another, not on her part at least. No other man had come close to satisfying her the way Charles had. Perhaps because she'd never allowed herself to get as emotionally involved with a man as she couldn't bear the pain that came with it, or perhaps because he'd been the best lover she'd ever had.

He knew exactly where to touch her to drive her crazy and exactly where she needed him to be. Charles too seemed to be making up for lost time, lust setting the heady rhythm of his every stroke inside her. It was as out of control as she'd ever seen him, or indeed had ever felt herself.

When her orgasm came it hit fast and hard, and as Charles's cries echoed hers she knew she never wanted this night to end. There was no more living in the past when the present was so much more enjoyable.

CHAPTER TWO

Two months later

EVERYTHING AND EVERYONE on this road trip had been telling Harriet to have a merry Christmas. From the radio presenters accompanying her on this journey, to the few strangers she'd encountered along the way, to the very weather, they'd been insisting she should be enjoying Christmas Day.

There was a fat chance of that happening, thanks to Charles, and now she was about to ruin his day too. She was happy to do this alone and more than capable. The only reason she was coming all this way was to give him the chance to step up to his obligations this time instead of walking away. He could tell her face to face if he didn't want any part of this, then they wouldn't have to see each other ever again.

The drive to Scotland had been long but uneventful thanks to the lull in traffic. Most people had chosen to stay at home celebrating with family and loved ones. How ironic when she had neither, but next year things would be different. Her whole life was about to change if she didn't take steps to secure the one she already had.

The closer she got to the Ross-Wylde family estate, the harder and faster her heart pounded and her stomach churned. Both from the conversation she had to have with Charles, and the last one they'd had at Heatherglen. She'd never imagined returning to the very place where she'd left her heart.

Road signs directed her towards the clinic that had essentially stolen Charles from her. Where he'd committed to setting up a life as the director there and Laird of the estate, instead of as her husband.

The drive up through the hills to her destination was as familiar to her as the last time she'd seen it, albeit through tear-filled eyes back then. It was dark now, the winter night so all-consuming it had swallowed up the colourful patchwork of countryside she knew surrounded her. All that remained were the inky shadows of the trees towering on either side of the winding road leading to Charles's ancestral home.

Buildings new and old appeared in view but her focus was entirely on the castle itself. With lights blazing in every window and the porch decorated with Christmas wreaths and garlands, it was a welcoming sight. An invitation to visitors that at least one of the residents might come to regret. She hadn't called or texted ahead so she had the element of surprise and could gauge Charles's true reaction to her news.

Harriet parked her car behind the others, which all had a dusting of snow like icing sugar on a sponge cake, and it was obvious no one had left the premises today. They'd been too busy having a good time, to judge by the sounds of music and laughter filtering through the crisp night air as she made her way to the entrance. There was a twinge of jealousy thinking of him celebrating the festive season here with family when she had no one. She rested her hand on her belly—flat for now. In another few months it would be a different story.

This wasn't about forcing him back into her life. She'd managed quite well without him these past years and she wasn't expecting anything from him now. Harriet wasn't that naïve. A baby hadn't been part of the deal, but she wanted to do the right thing by informing him of the pregnancy at least. With his track record she didn't believe he'd want to be involved and so she would let him know she didn't need anything from him. Her plan was simply to tell him and walk away, leaving them both with a clear conscience over the matter.

Before she could make her way up the stone steps, a door further along the castle burst open and all the warmth and excitement from inside spilled out.

'Oh, sorry. I didn't realise there was anyone out here. Are you here for the clinic?' The petite, smiling blonde looked familiar.

'Esme? Is that you?' She'd only been a teenager when Harriet had last seen her, but there was no doubt that was who she was looking at. It was those dazzling blue eyes, so much like her brother's, that gave away her identity.

'Yes? Can I help you?' There was no sign of recognition from the woman who'd almost been her sister-in-law but for all Harriet knew Charles could've had a procession of fiancées over the years. She couldn't be certain Esme would even remember her if she introduced herself.

'Esme, will you close the door, please? You're letting the cold in.' Charles's irritated voice sounded from inside right before he marched out to see what the commotion was on the doorstep.

It was then Harriet wondered what on earth she'd been thinking by turning up here tonight instead of waiting to speak to him on his own. In truth she hadn't been thinking clearly at all the second she'd seen the positive pregnancy test in her hand. She'd simply packed a bag and headed off to Scotland rather than spend the day considering what the consequences of their night of passion meant for her.

'Harriet?' He peered out into the darkness, glass of whisky in hand.

'Sorry. I didn't realise you'd have company.' She was prepared to walk away from the heated conversation she'd imagined having inside rather than discuss it in front of an audience.

'Harriet? Harriet Bell?' Esme let out a squeal and launched herself at Harriet, hugging her so tight she could no longer feel the cold, or much else.

'Esme, put her down.' Despite their more mature years, big brother Charles still spoke to her the way all boys did to their irritating little sisters. And, as all little sisters tended to do, Esme ignored him completely.

'What on earth are you doing here? It's been, what, ten years?' She had her arm around Harriet's shoulders now, steering her past the main entrance to the house to a side door.

'Twelve, but who's counting?' She managed to dodge answering the question when it was apparent Charles hadn't shared any details of even having met her at the convention. There should have been no reason for him to do so when they'd agreed to forget it had ever happened. Something they could no longer afford to do.

'It's good to see you.' Charles kissed her chastely on the cheek as she entered his ancestral home, probably for his sister's benefit. If he'd answered the door he might not have let her over the doorstep. This definitely hadn't been part of the arrangement.

'You too.' The brief contact was enough to fluster her and she hoped she could explain away her reddening skin with the cold.

'We use the main house for the clinic now. Esme and I have private rooms in another wing. We converted the old servants' quarters downstairs into a small kitchen and informal lounge. It affords us a little privacy from the comings and goings at the clinic. Now, can I get you a drink? A mulled wine or hot toddy to warm you up?' He swilled the contents of his whisky glass, filling the air with scent of cinnamon and warm spices.

'No, thanks. I'm driving. I'd take a cup of tea, though.' She didn't want anything, but she was hoping a trip to the kitchen would get her some privacy to speak to Charles alone.

'Ooh, what about a hot chocolate? I can make you a double chocolate with cream and marshmallows.' Esme's special sounded delicious after the poor service-station efforts they'd dared to charge Harriet for during the stops she'd made on the way here.

'That would be lovely, thank you.' This was all so civilised and bizarre. The Ross-Wyldes were acting as though she was a neighbour who'd just happened to drop by, not an ex-fiancée who'd turned up out of the blue after an extended absence. Either they were incredibly well mannered, which she knew, or they were too worried to ask why she'd come.

Lovely Esme slipped off towards the kitchen and Charles offered to take Harriet's coat for her. She supposed she was staying longer than she'd imagined.

'So, you were just passing by, huh?' He was smiling as he helped her out of her jacket.

She'd panicked when it was clear she couldn't blurt out the real reason she was here on his doorstep. He knew there was no 'just passing by' when London was an eight-hour drive away, yet he didn't seem put out by her unexpected arrival.

'I know this wasn't part of our deal and I'm sorry to intrude on you on Christmas night. I didn't realise you'd have a house full of people.' Even alluding to the 'arrangement' seemed salacious outside the anonymity of the hotel now, when they were in his home.

Charles, however, didn't appear perturbed if his smile was anything to go by. 'Oh, don't worry. You've saved me from another game of charades. Esme insists on covering all the clichés of the season.'

'That explains the outfit.' Now they were in better lighting she could see what he was wearing. The gold paper crown suited him, but the ugly sweater was a far cry from his usual dapper suits. Although he did look pretty cute in it.

'A present from little sis. She made it herself.' He rolled his eyes and Harriet knew he'd suffer the indignity of being seen in it rather than hurt Esme's feelings. If only he'd taken such consideration over *her* feelings when he'd broken up with her, she mightn't have been so intent on getting closure with that one last night together.

'That's lovely. It's so thoughtful for someone to put all that time and effort into making a gift.' To her, Christmas had become just another day. There weren't many presents beyond the odd box of chocolates or a bottle of wine from a grateful patient and she didn't bother making an elaborate Christmas dinner just for one. She preferred to work whenever she could, this year's exception giving her the chance to make the journey here.

'I guess. I'm sure she'd have made you one too if we'd known you were coming.'

Harriet could tell he was curious about what had brought her here when they'd severed all contact after that unforgettable night in his hotel room.

She cleared her throat. 'I came because there's something we need to discuss.'

'In that case, we should go somewhere quiet. We're winding down from our Christmas party and there are still a few people here.'

'That would be better.' She didn't want an audience for what was a very private matter.

'What are you two still doing, standing in the hall? Charles, bring Harriet in so she can have her hot chocolate by the fire.' Esme tutted as she chivvied them towards the lounge, but Charles resisted leaving the hallway.

'I think Harriet would prefer somewhere more peaceful after her long journey.'

She saw the disappointment on Esme's face and didn't want to hurt her feelings when she'd been so welcoming. 'I can always make time for a hot chocolate first.'

Charles seemed to understand what had brought on her change of heart and stood back to let them enter the living room in front of him.

There were a few couples engaged in conversation by the table of food along the back wall and a ruggedly handsome man, who got to his feet when he saw them, sitting by the fire.

'Harriet, this is Dr Max Kirkpatrick. Max,

this is Harriet Bell, an orthopaedic surgeon visiting from London.'

Charles made the introductions, giving little detail away, but Harriet realised it would be impolite for him to say she was the fiancée he'd dumped on inheriting the family silver. Introducing her as 'an ex I hooked up with recently at a medical conference' wouldn't have been the ideal ice-breaker either. The extra bodies in the room, however, did mean she was forced to delay her news a bit longer.

'Nice to meet you.' She shook hands with the man, who couldn't keep his eyes off Esme, and Harriet detected a reciprocal attraction between them. He wasn't the last man she remembered Esme being head over heels about, but she knew better than most that love didn't last for ever. These two still had that glow of new romance about them, which suggested they were in that phase when they found it hard to keep their hands off each other.

'You too. Esme, didn't you say you needed a hand with something in the kitchen?' Max wasn't very subtle about wanting some alone time with Esme, but Harriet didn't begrudge them their privacy. You had to take the good times when you could find them.

'Yes, I think I did.' Esme set the hot chocolate on the table and hurried out with him, giggling down the hall.

Harriet couldn't help but glance in Charles's direction, when they'd been as keen to spend time together not long ago. To find he was looking at her with that same longing was unravelling all the tension that had set in on the drive until her limbs felt more like spaghetti. One word and she just knew they'd both agree to another no-strings tryst. Except that word wouldn't be 'baby'. It was going to change the way he looked and felt about her, and probably not for the better.

'I should probably let you meet some of our staff here.' Charles led her over to the source of the chatter she'd heard from outside.

'Harriet Bell.' She shook hands with the group and introduced herself.

'Cassandra Bellow.' The pretty American set down the plate of canapés in her hand to greet her.

'Cassandra is one of our past patients and this is Lyle Sinclair, our medical director.' Charles didn't have to tell her these two were a couple either when they were glued to each other's sides.

'I'm Aksel Olson. I work with Esme.' The large hand pumping hers up and down next belonged to a bear of a man who couldn't fail to make an impression. The muscular build and Scandinavian accent coupled with the long air gave him a definite Viking vibe.

'Nice to meet you,' she said, before Charles moved her swiftly on to the woman standing next to him.

'Flora. I'm a physio at the clinic.'

'Hi.' She was definitely the gooseberry here but, then, so was Charles, who didn't seem to have a significant other in the mix. Something that hadn't gone unnoticed and brought her a sense of relief she hadn't known she needed. It hadn't entered her head that he might have met someone in the weeks since they'd last seen each other. Certainly, it hadn't been part of the deal that they couldn't date anyone else. They weren't supposed to see each other again. Thankfully, things wouldn't get any more complicated than they already were.

'And you've already met Esme and Max.' Charles didn't attempt to hide his disapproval as they reappeared with huge smiles on their faces.

'Are you staying in Cluchlochry?' Charles asked, as she attempted to drink her hot chocolate through the cream and marshmallow topping. It tasted as over-indulgent as it looked, and she just knew she was wearing a cream moustache as a result. As confirmed by Charles's smirk when she lifted her head to reply.

She did her best to wipe away all traces with the back of her hand. 'Probably. I didn't really think that far ahead.'

It would be suicidal to attempt a return trip tonight when she was ready for bed. There was bound to be a B&B in the village where she could put her head down for the night.

Charles frowned. 'Not everywhere would be willing to take guests in on Christmas night and those that do will be booked out. We get a lot of people who come for the

Christmas market and stay on for Christmas itself.'

'You must stay with us, Harri. There's plenty of room.' It was Esme who offered her refuge, not her brother. Although Harriet wanted to protest, she couldn't face getting back into her car again so soon.

'Esme, I really wish you wouldn't invite every waif and stray into Heatherglen as though it's your personal rescue centre. We converted the stables for your pet projects.'

'No offence taken,' Harriet muttered.

'Sorry. That was directed at someone else.' He nodded towards the furry bundle currently rolling around at his feet.

'Oh, he's gorgeous. What's his name?' She knelt down to stroke the curious-looking puppy with tiger-striped brown fur, which was wearing its own ugly little sweater.

'Dougal. He was half-starved when we found him, but Aksel nursed him back to health. Esme's trying to find him a home now.'

It was Flora who filled her in on his sad background, which just made him even more adorable.

'My sister has issues about turning anyone away.' Charles muttered.

'Harriet is neither a waif nor a stray. She's a friend who's very welcome to stay.' Esme overruled her older brother, using Harriet as a pawn in their sibling rivalry.

'I didn't say she wasn't. I was simply making a point, Esme.'

Harriet set down her cup. 'It would probably be easier if I look for somewhere in town to stay.'

This wasn't what she had planned at all. By this stage she'd expected to be on her way home, with Charles thanking his lucky stars for escaping the parent trap.

'No!' Both Ross-Wyldes expressed their indignation at the suggestion.

'I thought you said you wanted to talk to me about something?'

'We have so much catching up to do, Harri.'

The group watched the pair vying for her attention with as much fascination as she was, and Charles discreetly manoeuvred the argument away from the spectators over to the far side of the room.

'Charles is just trying to make a point—badly—about him being the king of the castle here. He runs the clinic and I run the veterinary practice and canine therapy centre across the way.' Esme punched him not so playfully on the arm.

'Oh, I think you mean Laird, Esme—but, yes, this isn't about you. Forgive me, Harriet. I'll take you up and show you to one of the spare rooms. Dear sister, perhaps you'd be so kind as to get Harriet something to eat too?'

He batted his eyelashes at Esme and Harriet knew it would be enough to persuade her to do anything. Especially when he was wearing those glasses and that jumper, which made him look more like the Charles she'd known instead of the suave version she'd met at the conference. She hoped that would keep some of the most recent, more erotic memories at bay so she could stay focused on the reason she'd come all this way.

'I would love to—but I'm doing it for our guest, not you, Chas.' Esme fluttered those same long dark eyelashes in response. They were so alike it was probably why they'd fought for as long as Harriet had known them. Deep down it was obvious how much they loved each other, and she wished she'd had a brother or a sister to fight with, love unconditionally, and have to hold after she'd lost everyone else.

'We keep a few rooms made up just in case of emergencies.' Charles led her up the stairs to one of the bedrooms. She couldn't help but wonder which door led to his.

'Do you get many late-night, uninvited women calling in on you?' she teased, when he was such a stark contrast to the man who'd literally sent her packing in a previous lifetime.

'No, I don't, but sometimes we get patients arriving too late to be admitted to the clinic, so we put them up here for the night.' Her teasing fell flat with him, but she supposed his defence from her insinuations was understandable when she was accusing him of having loose morals. She knew nothing about him any more.

'I'm sure it's most appreciated. As it is by me.' She had to remember he was doing her a favour by letting her stay when she had no right to be here. Their risky behaviour in London had been her idea and as such she was fully prepared to take on the consequences single-handedly.

'Bed, bathroom, wardrobe. All the essentials.' He did a quick tour of the room before turning back to her. 'Do you need help bringing in your luggage?'

'I just have an overnight bag in the car, but I can manage that myself. As I said, this was a spur-of-the-moment visit.'

'Ah, yes. The talk. Is this about what happened in London? I must admit it's been harder to put out of my mind than I'd imagined too.' He was moving towards her and Harriet's heart leapt into her throat at the thought of him kissing her again. She wanted it so much but that's not what had brought her here.

'I'm pregnant, Charles.'

His outstretched arms immediately fell limply to his sides. 'Pardon me?'

She sat down on the edge of the bed, wishing it would swallow her up. 'That night in London… I'm pregnant.'

Charles collapsed onto the mattress beside her. 'But—but we took precautions.'

'The first time,' she reminded him with as much of a smile as she could muster when she was wound up tighter than a drum, waiting for his reaction.

The second time had happened later, when they had both been naked under the covers and he'd reached for her, keen to do things at a slower pace and drive her wild with want before he had his way with her again. The third time, in the early hours of the morning, when she'd reached for him, knowing they would have to part again.

Conception could have happened at any point during those few passionate hours together. They'd simply been too wrapped up in each other, literally, to care. Well, they would now.

He dropped his head into his hands and she waited for him to process the information.

'Are you sure? Have you done a test?'

'Yes, Charles. I wouldn't have driven all this way otherwise.' She understood this was a shock to him, her too, but questioning her common sense wasn't going to make the situation go away.

'I gave up on plans for a family after we broke up. With very good reason. I don't have time to spare for babies and all the baggage that comes with them.' He was on his feet now, pacing the room like a caged animal. Trapped and unsure how to get out.

'Believe me, becoming a mother wasn't in my immediate plans either but here we are. I only came here to tell you about the baby because I thought it was the right thing to do. I didn't say I wanted anything from you. You had no room in your life for me, I wouldn't expect it to be different for your child.' If he thought she'd waited until she was at the peak of her career to seduce him, get pregnant and force him back into her life, he'd really forgotten who she was.

'That night was supposed to be a bit of fun. One last hurrah before we went our separate ways again. A baby means the complete opposite. We'll be tied together for ever now. If I'd wanted that I would've saved us the heartbreak of splitting up twelve years ago.'

'Okay. You've made your point. I don't think there's anything left for us to say.'

She should never have come here. Despite whatever flicker of hope she may have harboured for a different response, Charles had proved he hadn't changed. He still had the capacity to let her down. She'd managed this far on her own and she was sure she could raise this baby alone too. It was preferable to Charles feigning interest, only to have him bail out later and make their child suffer too.

Harriet was pregnant. It was his fault for not protecting her, for getting carried away, and not thinking about the consequences of his actions. Again.

When she'd turned up on the doorstep tonight he'd hoped it was because she'd wanted a replay of that night in London. Perhaps an extended version that would have taken them into the New Year instead of one night. Mostly because he hadn't been able to get that time together out of his head, but this was a whole different scenario.

He was waiting, hating this ridiculous sweater more than ever, for Harriet to give him some sort of clue what he was supposed to do next. Instead, she slowly rose from the bed, crossed the floor and walked out the door. It wasn't the response he'd expected but some space would be good. Esme could keep her entertained and when he'd digested the news they could sit down and plan the next move.

Any second now Esme would come bowling up the stairs and deliver a knock-out punch once she heard what had happened. He was surprised Harriet hadn't done just that after the way he'd spoken to her. It had been a knee-jerk reaction to finding out he was going to be a father and one he'd apologise for once this sank in. He was angry at himself, not her, when his selfish needs had resulted in this life-changing news. The last thing he'd ever wanted to do was complicate her life.

Harriet's response to his outburst was reminiscent of that awful day of his father's funeral. She hadn't slapped him then either, the way most women would have. Silently crying, she'd simply packed her things and walked out. He hadn't seen or heard from her again until that conference.

At the sound of a car engine running outside, Charles rushed to the window in time to see Harriet driving away. It was déjà vu, except he couldn't claim his actions, or lack of them now, had been in any way for her benefit.

'Charles, what the hell have you done?' Esme arrived, as he'd known she would, temper flaring, fists balling, ready for a fight.

'Not now.'

'You must have said something to make her leave like that. Are you really just going to stand here and watch her go? Again?' That was the ultimate question. What they were going to do about the baby, how he felt about Harriet and what they did next were incidental if he let her go without a fight again. She was a successful surgeon in her own right with no need for him or his money. He was the one standing to lose out here.

'Tell everyone to go home. The party's over.' He left Esme to break up the gathering before dashing downstairs to retrieve his own car keys. His child wasn't going to grow up thinking its father was a disappointment, like the rest of his family had.

This was one time he could do the right thing without waiting until it was too late. He couldn't live with any more guilt and regret. Losing his father and brother had taught him not to be selfish, and unless he wanted to lose his child too he had to think about the needs of its mother. That didn't include being upset by her baby's father. Not when she'd driven the whole way to Scotland to tell him personally on Christmas Day. Something a person would only do if they had no one else to turn to.

CHAPTER THREE

'DID YOU HONESTLY expect him to react any differently? What were you hoping for? A happy-ever-after? Stupid woman!' Harriet chastised herself in the mirror as she drove away.

She'd given him the chance to be involved in the baby's life and he wasn't interested. End of story. It was his loss. She knew where she stood and that wasn't with Charles by her side. She could raise this child alone. It would be better for her and the child. At least it was apparent she'd be parenting on her own from the beginning, unlike her poor mother.

Coming here had been a reminder that night in London had been nothing more than a fantasy. The real Charles was entrenched in family tradition and duty with no room for anyone else in his life. Harriet was an independent city girl. She didn't belong here. She hated the fact it still hurt that he didn't want her, whatever the circumstances.

Perhaps she'd convinced herself something had changed between them after their escapade in that hotel room, and not merely on a physical level. Deep down she'd hoped he'd be pleased to see her again because, even before realising she was pregnant, she'd wondered about rekindling their relationship. Sentimentality and lust over common sense, but she hadn't been thinking with her head lately. That's how she'd ended up in this mess.

Charles Ross-Wylde had altered the course of her life again, sending her down a road she'd never planned to take. Now she simply had to make the best of it, the way she had the last time. Only instead of becoming a successful surgeon, her next goal was to become a good mother too.

Bright lights began strobing around her, disturbing the pitch-black night. A glance in her rear-view mirror revealed a car, flashing its headlights at her and now blaring its horn.

Someone from the house had followed her and was trying to get her attention. Esme, no doubt, had figured out something was amiss and was coming to persuade her to go back. There was no way Charles would've told his sister about the baby when he didn't want it messing up his life. It was likely to be her good heart making her chase after someone who was virtually a stranger now.

Although Harriet had no intention of going back with her, she would put Esme's mind at ease because she held no bad feelings towards her. She indicated and pulled into the side of the road. The sooner they said their goodbyes, the sooner she could leave Heatherglen behind her for ever.

She stepped out onto the grass verge, but the headlights continued to blind her as she waited for the driver to get out. It wasn't until the very tall, very male silhouette drew closer that she realised it wasn't Esme who'd flagged her down.

'I have nothing to say to you. At least, nothing very ladylike,' she threw at Charles, hurrying back towards her car. He probably wanted her to sign some sort of gagging order to prevent her from claiming her unborn child had any right to the estate.

Her attempt to open her car door was thwarted as Charles grabbed her arm and spun her around. 'I'm sorry, Harriet. I reacted badly.'

'You think?' She tried to wrench her arm out of his grasp. It was going to be harder to continue hating him if he insisted on touching her, reminding her of an intimacy they could never have again.

'Come back to the house so we can talk.' He didn't let go of her, but he did loosen his grip.

'Why? You've made it clear you don't want to be part of this.'

'I'm sorry. It was a shock to the system, that's all. We both know I was a very willing participant that night, and the following morning.' His cheeky grin did things to her insides, which apparently shouldn't be acted on.

Goodness, she needed him to stop teasing her with enough delicious memories to block out the more hideous ones. Twice now he'd let her down in the most callous way. The last time she'd forgotten not to trust him and had let her hormones do the talking she'd ended up pregnant.

'I should've called instead of coming here.' That was one thing she was sure about and something he'd agree with when she'd spoiled his Christmas.

'No. I'm glad you came. Look, it's late and freezing cold out here. Why don't you just come back to the house? The talking can wait.'

It was tempting when her stomach was rumbling and the tip of her nose was so cold she was convinced it had turned blue. She thought of the lovely roaring fire in the lounge and the banquet of food spread out and going to waste. Pregnancy apparently had lowered the price of her pride. If she went back with him it would be for the baby's sake. They had things to sort out. It was the whole reason she was here. It definitely wasn't anything to do with the man still holding her, dressed in that ridiculous sweater his little sister had knitted for him.

'I don't have anywhere else to go, I suppose.' She didn't fancy traipsing around town, knocking on doors and hoping to find room at an inn.

'That's settled, then. You're coming home with me.' If only he meant that as something other than a polite host she'd be reassured he'd had a change of heart where the baby was concerned. This was more about him saving face in front of his family and friends. She shouldn't get too carried away with the idea that he'd finally stepped up to be the man she'd always believed he was deep down. For now, she'd take advantage of the food and lodgings being offered because it suited her and meant she'd no longer be putting her unborn child at risk out here in the Scottish wilderness.

'Fine.' She got back into her car, but nothing had changed. Except perhaps his conscience getting the better of him at letting the mother of his child disappear into the night.

Harriet followed Charles back to the house, resolving to take herself straight to bed and avoid any further confrontation. When he slammed on his brakes as they approached the house, she almost ran into the back of his car. As it was, she nearly gave herself whiplash having to make her own emergency stop.

'What the hell are you playing at, Charles?' she shouted as she wrestled her seat belt off, about to jump out and give him hell. That's when she saw him bolting across the driveway, not even taking time to close the car door behind him.

She got out and followed him over to the side of the road where the house lights didn't quite manage to reach. It wasn't until she was standing over him that she realised what it was his headlights had picked up along the drive. Charles was hunched over the body of a woman who was clearly having some sort of fit. Stranger still, there was a dog lying next to her, providing some sort of cushion for her head.

'Fenella? Can you hear me? It's Charles, Esme's brother.' Charles checked the woman's pulse while he tried to get some sort of response from her.

Harriet knelt beside them and brushed away the debris of Christmas presents scattered around her, and anything else she could hurt herself on while her body was jerking uncontrollably on the cold ground. 'Is she one of your patients?'

'One of Esme's clients. She's epileptic so we'll just have to wait this out with her.'

When someone was having a seizure it was important not to restrain or try to move them in case of injury. All they could do was make sure she didn't hurt herself and time the fitting in case it developed into something more serious. A fit lasting more than five minutes could lead to brain damage.

'I don't think she hurt herself in the fall. I can't see any obvious injuries.' Harriet checked as best she could and loosened the scarf around Fenella's neck.

'That'll be down to Nora, the dog Esme trained with her. She would've alerted Fenella that the seizure was coming and positioned herself underneath to prevent her hitting her head.'

'That's amazing.' She'd known what Esme did for a living but actually seeing it in practice made Harriet see what a valuable service she was providing to the people who came to her. As was Charles. Despite her personal issues with him, there was no denying the good he was doing at Heatherglen between the clinic and the canine therapy centre he'd set up with his sister.

'The convulsions are slowing now. She should be back with us soon.'

'I'll go and alert the others so we can get her inside out of this cold.' Harriet hurried inside to inform Esme and Max so they could organise a transfer for her into the clinic. When she came round, Fenella would be tired and probably confused about what had happened. She'd be spending the night under medical observation and so would Nora.

By the time Fenella had been admitted to a bed in the clinic for the night and Esme had taken Nora to the kennels, Harriet was emotionally and physically exhausted. Charles had gone out to park the cars and lock them so she thought she could sneak off to bed unnoticed.

With a foot on the first tread of the staircase she thought she'd got away with it until Charles called her back.

'Harriet, you don't have to hide away from me up there. Come and get something to eat. You deserve it after the night you've had.'

Her stomach rumbled and made the decision to stay for her. 'I did miss dinner.'

'It's important for the baby's sake that you don't skip meals.' At least he was acknowledging her condition, even if it was only to scold her.

The house was unfeasibly quiet compared to the raucous atmosphere she'd arrived to earlier. 'Is Fenella okay?'

Charles led her to the kitchen where the worktops were laden with covered leftovers. 'She'll be fine. Apparently, she was coming to deliver a few Christmas presents to the staff but she really shouldn't have been out walking alone in that cold weather. I'm going to look into the medication she's on and see if I can reduce the frequency of the seizures. I'll get onto Clydesbank Hospital again and get a rush on her records. In the meantime, Esme is spoiling the dog something rotten for doing such a good job tonight.' The smile on his face showed the pride he had in his sister's achievements.

'Does Esme know about you-know-what?' She pointed to her belly, afraid to mention the baby again and end this fragile truce, but she didn't want to put her foot in it if she ran into Esme at some point.

'No. One thing at a time. Now, turkey sandwich?' He uncovered the carcass of their earlier dinner and Harriet was so hungry she could've attacked it with her bare hands.

'Yes, please.'

'Help yourself to a drink.' He waved the huge carving knife in the direction of the fridge, where she found a bottle of non-alcoholic grape fizz. She poured two glasses in the hope he wasn't just going to sit there and watch her eat. Thankfully, he placed two plates of sandwiches on the table and they both sat down.

'This is really good. Thanks, Charles.'

'I'm sorry about what I said earlier, Harriet.'

After a couple of bites, they talked over each other, Charles surprising her with his topic of choice.

'You were being honest. A baby isn't in your plans.'

He set down his half-eaten sandwich. Harriet's appetite too had waned at the reminder of their earlier conversation. 'It's been a long day and I wasn't prepared for that kind of bombshell. I shouldn't have been so short with you.'

'Believe me, it came as a shock to me too. Why do you think I jumped into my car and started driving here, Charles? I didn't know how to react any more than you do, but the important thing is where we go from here.'

An apology for his behaviour on this occasion was progress and more than he'd offered the last time he'd spoken to her so harshly.

'Okay, so you're a couple of months gone?'

She nodded, though she'd been so busy she hadn't noticed the first missed period. 'I honestly only came to tell you about the baby so no one could ever say I kept it from you. I mean, joint parenting between London and Scotland simply isn't feasible. Plus, I intend to continue with my medical career.' Motherhood and her job could co-exist if organised properly well in advance.

Charles took a drink as he contemplated his response. 'I want to *be* a father. I just didn't think it would happen. Although seeing everyone around me settling down and starting their own families has made me realise I did want that once. I know this wasn't planned, but it's really a blessing. I mean, this child will be the heir to Heatherglen. This is a legacy that should be passed on to the next generation. I can't let you walk away with my baby when I'd want to be more than just a weekend dad. Family is everything to me and I want my child close.'

It was such a turnaround Harriet's head was spinning. She should've considered the Ross-Wylde obsession with family tradition before coming here. Of course the Laird of Heatherglen would want an heir and she'd made it all so easy for him. There was nothing to say he had to want her along with the baby. As was clear when his first thoughts were about passing on his legacy. She'd left herself open to becoming collateral damage for a second time.

Did Charles think he could somehow get custody of their child and keep her out of the picture altogether? She hadn't anticipated having a custody fight on her hands but if he insisted, she'd do everything in her power to make sure this child had a stable influence in life. Experience had taught her that Charles wasn't reliable enough for that role.

'How do you suppose we do that? It's not practical for either of us to travel up and down the country on a whim and my schedule is not nine to five, Monday to Friday. What are you going to do, kidnap me? Lock me up in the attic until I give birth and dispose of me when I've outlived my usefulness?' She snorted. It might sound absurd but right now he was making her feel little more than a baby-making machine. This wasn't supposed to be about him. She had to fit in a life of her own somewhere, not spend every spare minute making sure Charles was happy.

'I don't think we need to resort to that, but you could move in here. The house is big enough that we could live our separate lives and share child care.' He'd managed to come up with a practical solution to co-parenting that suited him. Her initial suspicion was that he'd only suggested the move because he knew she'd never agree to it. Heatherglen held so many sad associations for her that she couldn't imagine waking up every morning in the very place where their fairy-tale romance had turned into a nightmare.

Then he would be free to make a legal bid for custody and who wouldn't think a child would be better off with his prestigious side of the family and their millions in the bank? A cold sweat broke out over Harriet's skin at the fight she could have on her hands for a baby she hadn't realised she wanted so much until now.

'You know that's not an option, Charles. My life and my career are in London.' Unlike him, she'd never left.

'Hear me out. The country would be so much better to raise a child than the city. You have no family there and look at the land we have around us. At least here you'd be surrounded by family and friends.'

'Your family, your friends, your home and your rules, I expect.' She wasn't going to let him control her. There was no way she was giving up her independence to be locked away in a tower, so the Laird and master of all he surveyed had unlimited access to his heir. What was in that for her?

'Esme would be the baby's family too. Everyone else who lives and works at Heatherglen would soon become a friend to you. Not to mention those mutts my sister keeps around the place. I'm sure a child would appreciate growing up around her four-legged friends much more than I do.' There was a hint of tension surrounding the matter and she could imagine how irked he'd be finding puppies peeing on his antique rugs. She'd be tempted to agree just to see his face when that happened.

'I told you, I'm not flushing away my career because I'm pregnant. Being the mother of your children is no longer enough for me in life, as hard as that might be for you to believe.' His ego had grown to match the size of his bank balance if he thought he was enough for her to turn her back on the success she'd worked so hard to achieve.

'I'm not asking you to give anything up for me. It would be for the baby.'

'Emotional blackmail won't get you anywhere, Charles. I'll raise this child to understand women can have it all these days. You did me a favour, you know, dumping me like that. If you hadn't, I would've left London there and then and moved here with you. I would never have had the career I have now.'

'Why do you think I did it?' he mumbled as he cleared the dishes away. That was the first time he'd offered any explanation for his actions, but he wasn't making any sense.

'You told me you no longer wanted to marry me, that you had Heatherglen and didn't need me once you inherited your father's land and title.' Not his exact words but it was the gist of his rejection after his father's funeral and sufficient to send her back to London alone with a broken heart.

'Did you honestly believe I was able to switch off my feelings for you so easily? I knew you'd insist on moving back here with me and I didn't want you to give up on your medical dreams. This place cost my father his life. I knew the mess and the hard work I had waiting for me here. I didn't want to inflict that suffering on you too.'

Harriet could see he was being sincere and felt as though her heart was breaking all over again. For that young woman who'd believed she wasn't good enough for the love of her life, and for the grieving son who'd had the weight of the world on his shoulders.

'I had no idea.' Her voice was but a whisper as she came to terms with the knowledge it had all been a lie, albeit with the best of intentions. All these years she'd hated him when he'd acted out of love for her. Yet there was a slow burning fire starting deep inside her that he'd taken the choice away from her about her future.

'Yes, well, we can't go back even if we wanted to. This is about moving forward.'

'Wait. You made that decision for me to return to London and now you're dictating I move here because it's more convenient for you? Control freak much? Are you so bored and lonely out here you've decided it might be nice to have an ex with benefits on site?' She couldn't sit here any more when she wanted to smash things, including Charles's face, for he was being so damned noble and breaking her heart without giving her a valid reason. There was no doubt she would've moved to Heatherglen with him because she'd loved him and nothing else had mattered. It was a shame he hadn't felt the same way about her.

'I know you're angry, but it worked out for the best, didn't it? Until now.' He gave a sad smile, which she wasn't sure was for her or himself.

It was a revelation to find out his behaviour, in his eyes, had been in her best interests. From the outside it would seem his plan had worked. She was financially stable, living in London with a career she'd dreamed of, but she'd never been able to trust again. Despite his scheming, fate had brought them together in the end, expecting the baby she'd always imagined having with Charles. Except now the circumstances didn't include parents who were in love or anything like it.

'My career isn't up for negotiation.' She wasn't budging on that point and he couldn't make her. If he had sent her away to build on her career, that time apart would've been wasted if she was expected to give it all up now.

'We have the clinic here. It would be a real coup to have someone of your calibre with us. Heatherglen could offer you a flexible position to fit around your needs and a home for you and the baby. Come and work here. It sounds like the perfect solution to me.'

'Of course it does. You win this way. It's your home and it doesn't inconvenience you. You get to play daddy on a full-time basis on your doorstep and get an orthopaedic surgeon thrown in too. However, it's asking a lot from me to give up everything at home to move here.' Regardless of Charles's wealth and the unspoilt land around Heatherglen, Harriet didn't know if this was the best environment in which to raise a child, or even to live in herself. She knew nothing of life in the country or how isolated she might feel here. However, she did know that Heatherglen hadn't brought her happiness in the past and the family ties that kept Charles here weren't what she wanted for her baby.

What scared her most, though, was having all those feelings resurfacing for Charles and being trapped here with them. One night had been difficult enough to forget, even before she'd realised she had a souvenir of the event.

'It's not a competition, Harriet. Don't you want us to do this together? It would be a partnership without the inconvenient distance between us.' He made it sound so straightforward, but it was that distance that would keep her sane now they were back in each other's lives.

'Do you really have need for an orthopaedic surgeon here? I mean, I'm not trading in a full schedule for the odd consultation here and there. I'm not taking a demotion.' The whole point of this exercise was to ensure parenting wouldn't affect her working life. She couldn't help thinking this was going to end up with her in that stay-at-home mum role she was trying to avoid.

'As a matter of fact, I have a patient at the moment I could use your help with. If you find clinic life and motherhood aren't enough for you, I'm sure every hospital within a hundred-mile radius will be queuing up to have you on their books. You could consult, run your own clinics. Whatever you need.' He was being so damned reasonable it was difficult to argue with the options he was laying out before her. It was being around other people she found most appealing. Life in London was busy, hectic, and she did everything at breakneck speed, but that was because she didn't have anyone at home to make it worth her while to slow down to enjoy time out from it all. That was going to change in a few months, whether she was ready for it or not.

'Why should I believe you're not going to change your mind again?' There was no way of predicting the outcome if she took this gamble but there was every chance she'd be the one to come off worse out of this arrangement.

'I've lost a brother, a father and a fiancée because of this place. I don't want it to cost me the chance of being a father too. You know I can't leave here, there's just too much responsibility involved, but I want my child to know I'll be there for her or him. Your moving here would give me the chance to do that.'

'It's a lot to put on my shoulders, Charles, and after everything we've been through...'

'Marry me, then. I can provide you both with everything you could ever need. I know you need something in return to offset everything you'd be trading in to come here.'

'Don't be ridiculous.' It was like a slap across the face for him to toss a proposal of marriage in there so casually, as if it meant nothing, when the last time he'd asked her that question it had meant the world to her.

Her mother had passed away not long after they'd started dating and Charles had represented everything she'd thought she'd have in her new life. Marriage and stability were all she'd wanted then but he had obviously never held it in the same regard when he'd used it as a device to keep her dangling on a string.

'It's not unheard of for a couple to get married for the sake of a baby. I would give you equal rights to the estate, the clinic and anything else you wanted.' He was offering everything except love and devotion, the only things that could ever convince Harriet marriage would be a good idea.

'No.'

His shoulders slumped when she torpedoed his marriage of convenience idea, but he'd a lot to learn about the woman he was dealing with now. This one wouldn't be so easily swayed into the life-changing decisions he made on a whim.

'When are you due back at work?'

'Not until January. Why?'

'You could spend the rest of your break here. A trial run if you like. You could get to know the staff and patients at the clinic and see where you could be working if you gave it a chance.'

'See if you and I can live together in the same place without coming to blows?' She didn't know how to get out of this situation she'd created by coming here in the first place. If she left now, Charles would be sure to look into the legalities surrounding the baby's parentage and she didn't want him or her to get caught in a tug of war between them. It might be best to do as he'd suggested and stay. That way she could do her best to make him see how impossible it would be for her to fit in here. She would be reasonable and, when it didn't work out, she could say she'd tried to do things his way. Once she was back in London and the baby was born it would be too unsettling for them to uproot again.

If she stayed, it wouldn't be the clashes between them she was sure would keep her awake at night but the memories of the passion he'd awakened in her. Something she'd be reminded of with every ounce of gained weight and growing belly. Yet he'd barely mentioned that incredible time they'd had, as if it had never happened, and this pregnancy had been some sort of divine intervention.

This baby had apparently been created from thin air solely to provide him with the opportunity to become a father. A few days under the same roof would give them both an idea of how difficult it would be to carry on that pretence. If she couldn't manage it, they'd have to come up with a plan B. For now, this was the only one they'd come up with.

'What do you say, Harriet? You, me and baby for the rest of the festive season? It would mean you'll be here for our Hogmanay party too. Esme is hosting it this year so it's sure to be a spectacle you don't want to miss.'

She tried to convince herself it was the headache of facing a custody battle that finally persuaded her to stay. Not his smiling blue eyes or the thought of them spending time as a family.

CHAPTER FOUR

'ORANGE JUICE, CEREAL, toast and tea.' Charles ticked off the breakfast checklist as he loaded a tray to take up to Harriet. Since it was early in her pregnancy, he wasn't sure how she'd react faced with a cooked breakfast first thing in the morning and chose the safe option.

He still couldn't quite believe he was going to be a father. For the longest time it had only been him and Esme at the castle, wrapped up in their own careers. Now there would be a new focus. Okay, the suggestion of marriage had been a mistake but since he and Harriet had agreed back in London that they had no future together, he'd wanted something to keep her in his life. He was asking her to give up more than ever to move back to Scotland now, with nothing to offer her in return. For now he just wanted time with her and a chance for them to work this out together.

Family was something he never dared believe he could have after inheriting Heatherglen and knowing his whole life would be tied up in it. It was expected for the Laird to marry and provide an heir, but it had been more important for him to get the clinic up and running. Now he had no choice, and there was going to be a baby, it was a chance for him to be normal and have a role for himself other than running the castle and clinic. No other woman had lived up to Harriet, so it seemed only fitting that she should be the mother of his child.

'Someone looks happy this morning.'

He looked up to find Harriet standing in the kitchen doorway with much the same expression on her face as the one he was wearing.

'I was thinking how nice it might be to have a wee one running around the place.' He didn't need to lie to her when he was trying to persuade her to stick around. She had to know he was looking forward to it all, no longer fighting the idea.

'I haven't agreed to anything yet.' Her frown told him he'd jumped the gun, but he was determined to make her see this was the best place for them both.

'What are you doing up, anyway? I was going to bring you breakfast in bed.' He did his best to dodge another argument, even though he was miffed she'd thwarted his attempt to gain brownie points.

'I'm an early riser. I like to make the most of every day. Thanks, though.' She took a seat at the table and started picking at a slice of toast from the tray. Charles joined her so he wouldn't appear rude in leaving her by herself, then poured himself a cup of coffee and sat down.

'Ah, yes. My little lark. I'd forgotten how much you enjoy mornings.' It was a throwaway comment borne of past familiarity, but it brought back more recent, erotic memories, which made him shift in his chair. Images of their early morning tryst in that hotel bed burst into his thoughts and refused to leave.

Harriet was blinking at him, her toast hovering in mid-air, frozen by the inappropriate reference to her insatiable appetite for him. It wasn't as though they could avoid the subject altogether when she was carrying the evidence, but he realised he'd been indiscreet. Harriet had made it clear she didn't intend to let their past get in the way of a potential working relationship.

'It's only me!' Esme's timely arrival through the back door saved both their blushes.

'Morning, Esme.' Harriet sounded as relieved as he was to have someone break the sudden tension in the air.

His sister was going to lose her mind when she heard she was going to be an aunt.

'I've just been down to the therapy centre to pick up a few things. Charles said you could use a change of clothes so you didn't get yours dirty. I brought you some of our winter gear.' She plonked the pile of clothes and boots on the table, Charles whipping away the breakfast things a fraction of a second before she did so.

'That's very kind of you but there's really no need to fuss.'

'It's only a sweater, some waterproofs and a pair of wellies to wear around the estate. Nothing fancy, just practical.'

Harriet made no further protest. 'Thank you. I don't know how much longer I'll get away with wearing my own clothes anyway.'

She tested the give in the trousers, stretching the elastic waistband. Charles could see the very second she realised what she'd said as her wide-eyed gaze flicked between him and Esme.

His sister didn't miss it either. 'What do you mean?'

Worried he'd put his foot in it more than he already had, Charles left it to Harriet as to what to say next. There would be no going back once Esme knew about the baby. Although, by the excitement he could already see fizzing up inside her, she'd probably already guessed.

'I...er...' Harriet cleared her throat. 'I'm pregnant.'

Esme managed to contain herself a second or two longer until Harriet confirmed the paternity, should it be in question.

'Charles is the father.'

His sister's squeal almost deafened him. 'Oh, my goodness! When did this happen? How did this happen? Wait…don't answer that one. This. Is. *Amazing!*'

Another squeal and she launched herself at Harriet. Charles leaned back against the kitchen worktop, content to let them hug it out, only to have the breath knocked out of him too by an Esme missile.

'Are you trying to kill me?' He laughed as she squeezed him hard.

'I'm just so happy for you, bro.' She paused. 'It is good news, isn't it?'

He supposed neither he nor Harriet appeared to have as much zing as the auntie-to-be.

'Yes, of course.' There was no hesitation in his reply and he wished he'd been as positive about the news the first time around. That knee-jerk, defensive lashing out had damaged what little trust Harriet had left in him, but he hoped he'd have the chance to repair their relationship over these next few days. If only for the baby's sake.

'It was that conference, wasn't it? I knew something had happened. You couldn't wipe the smile off your face for a week. My brother has been emotionally frozen since losing you, unless you count being perpetually grumpy. You're the one person who ever seemed to make him happy.' Esme knew him better than he was comfortable with and the heat in his cheeks confirmed he'd flushed the same shade of scarlet as Harriet.

He flashed Harriet an unspoken apology for his sibling's lack of tact. This was their love life, the supposedly never-to-be-spoken-of-again fling they were now discussing over the breakfast table. A bit much for someone who hadn't set foot in this house in over a decade.

'I'm only here over the festive season so we can work a few things out.' If Harriet didn't see the need to satisfy Esme's curiosity with the details, neither would he.

'Well, I hope you do. Feel free to pop down to the therapy centre and look around or, you know, if you just want to talk.' As subtle as a brick, Esme shot a dark look in his direction that said she'd already pinpointed him as the source of their conflict. He'd prepare himself for an interrogation, followed by an ear-bashing, once they were alone.

'Thanks. I'll keep that in mind.'

'Yes, Esme, thanks for bringing the clothes over for Harriet. We wouldn't want to keep you from your work any longer than necessary.' He didn't need her siding against him too if she thought he'd been in the wrong. Which he had been. Besides, he needed every second he could get alone with Harriet to try and redeem himself.

'It's lovely to have you here, Harriet.' Esme ignored him and kissed her new favourite person—which obviously wasn't him—on the cheek.

'I'm only a couple of months gone, so I'd appreciate it if you keep the news to yourself for now.' It might've helped Charles's cause if Harriet hadn't enforced a news blackout, but he knew Esme would respect her wishes, even if she was fit to bust with the good news.

'I can't believe I'm going to be an auntie.' She skipped back out the door and he envied her carefree position in this situation.

'She's going to make a wonderful aunt,' Harriet mused.

'Esme will spoil the baby rotten.' She was bad enough fussing over those dogs so the second a baby was on the scene the place would be filled with toys and cute outfits. Strangely, the thought of the castle being turned upside down didn't disturb him as much as it usually did. It would be nice for it to be a proper home again instead of a memorial reminding him of everything he'd lost. His sister was right about one thing, though. He had been frozen here, never really coming to terms with his losses, including Harriet. Hopefully now, reconnecting with her would bring him some peace again.

'Yes, well, I'm sure we'll be glad to have an extra pair of hands when it comes to babysitting. *If* I decide to stay.' Harriet was quick to correct herself, but it was a good sign she was thinking about having support here at Heatherglen rather than being on her own. Letting the news slip to Esme could've been the best thing to happen. For him. With his sister on side he'd have double the chance of persuading Harriet to stay permanently.

'Why don't I give you a tour of the clinic and let you see everything we've achieved?' Perhaps if she saw why he'd sacrificed their future it would give them the chance to have another one.

Harriet cursed her big mouth. As lovely as Esme was, she wished she hadn't blabbed about the pregnancy. Now there was more than her and Charles involved it was bound to complicate things. Once Charles realised there was no way she was letting him dictate the rest of her and her baby's lives, a clean break wasn't going to be so easy. Not with a super-excited auntie in the mix.

She could do without Charles being all charming and thoughtful too. He'd thrown her last night by coming after her and begging her to stay. Even if it was for his own selfish reasons. That last-minute plea for a second chance, that offer of a future here at Heatherglen had left an opening for a flicker of hope she couldn't extinguish that he might still be the honourable gentleman she'd once believed him to be.

Their time together at that conference

had reawakened feelings for Charles she had no business having when he didn't deserve them. She had confused past Harriet and Charles for their present-day incarnations because her hormones were all over the place.

So, she'd woken up this morning determined to harden her heart against him. Only to find him making her breakfast, smiling to himself about the baby coming, and arranging for her to be more comfortable in this environment. That's why she'd spilled the beans to Esme. She'd been so comfortable she'd started imagining being here as part of a family.

All she could do to save herself now as he led her out for a walk in the grounds was to look at Heatherglen from a professional viewpoint. There was no way she'd be content with swapping the hustle and bustle of London hospitals for a country practice. Working on a casual basis in the middle of nowhere would be a demotion for her. A sure-fire way to ensure her career took a back seat to motherhood. Exactly what she'd hoped to avoid.

'I know the twenty-sixth of December is considered a holiday, but I hope you don't mind if I call in and see my patients? It must suck, being away from home at this time of year.'

They walked to the front of the clinic and it seemed odd to find everything still decorated for the season when Christmas Day had been something of a non-event for her. Christmas night, on the other hand, had been more action-packed than she'd anticipated.

'I don't mind at all. I know as well as you do we're never really off duty.' If she'd been back in London she might've been calling in on some of her own patients. There weren't very many people in her life. At least, none who'd be spending time with her instead of with their own families.

Sometimes those patients having treatment were her comfort as much as she hopefully was theirs. Hospital could be a lonely place with only sporadic visitors, if any. Much like her home life. A simple chat could reassure both sides there was life outside those four walls.

'Sorry, I didn't mean to be insensitive.' It

took her a few seconds to figure out what he was apologising for. He'd mistakenly believed she might have been pining for the comfort of her own home when it was strangers in a different medical setting she had been thinking about. Not that she was going to have him pity her by explaining that to him.

He'd given up their relationship to remain here, transforming an ancestral pile into somewhere he and his sister could work and live side by side. Home was never somewhere he'd leave when he'd given up everything to keep it. Whereas her apartment was simply a base where she slept between surgeries and meetings. It could literally be anywhere in the world. Easily transferable. There was no real emotional connection. If that's what constituted a home, there was more attachment for her at Heatherglen already.

'Don't worry about it. There'll be plenty more Christmases to come.' Once there was a baby involved, things would be different. She was sure she'd want to spend all the time she could with her child rather than wandering around hospital wards.

It had been a long time since she'd felt the excitement other people seemed to draw from Christmas and she was looking forward to experiencing it for herself. Whether it was London or here at Heatherglen, Harriet knew next year would be the best one yet.

'Things might have changed since you were last here.' Charles showed off the renovations with pride, but Harriet couldn't view his achievements objectively when she knew they'd come at the price of her happiness. Every new fixture and fitting had been built on her heartache.

'So, how many patients do you take in at a time?'

'We can manage around twenty residents, but Esme deals with more clients at the therapy centre. We've got a good set-up.'

They wandered past a Christmas tree decorated similarly to the one in the private wing except it was missing those personal touches of home-made ornaments she was sure were Esme's handiwork.

'Didn't this used to be—?' She spun around, finding something familiar about the space they were in, except in place of the heavy velvet drapes she recalled, there were modern vertical blinds.

'Ah, yes, this used to be the lounge. We had to replace a lot for health and safety reasons, but we tried to keep the original features, like the fireplace. This one is only for the aesthetics now.' It remained grand and ornate in here, although it had been re-purposed, but it was in this very room he'd crushed her thoughts of marrying him.

Perhaps that was why he'd gutted it. In the hope of removing all traces of her and what had happened. This place was proof that wasn't possible. You couldn't simply erase history because it suited you. There were always going to be reminders of the past intruding on the present, no matter how hard you tried to cover it up.

'I remember being in here the day of your father's funeral.' She hadn't said it to upset him. The memory of that day, the room full of people and chatter as they'd mourned his loss, was simply too vivid to ignore. It had been clear something other than grief had been plaguing Charles when he'd been so distant they could've been in different cities then instead of standing side by side. He'd done her the courtesy of waiting until the other mourners had departed before he'd ended their engagement, even insisting she keep the ring, but it hadn't lessened her humiliation or confusion.

'It was a long time ago.' Something he obviously didn't want to be reminded of when he was striding on towards the other rooms.

Harriet bit her lip when it wasn't as easy for her to dismiss it but opening up old wounds wasn't going to help either of them. She was supposed to be over it all, that's what she'd told him, or he'd probably never have slept with her again. They couldn't change what had happened then any more than they could alter their decisions, or lack of them, in London.

She wasn't sure he'd even do anything differently when so many had benefitted from the clinic since their break-up. Certainly, she wouldn't choose to change more recent events between them. Motherhood wasn't something she'd wish away now when it was a part of her. If she hadn't fallen pregnant by accident she might never have factored a baby into her life and she had no regrets about the prospect of becoming a mum. It was the most important event in her life she had to look forward to. They simply had to live with the decisions they'd made and make the most of whatever fate had in store for them.

'So, what services do you offer here?' Back onto more neutral ground, perhaps she'd stop getting so emotional about what this place represented to her and begin to see it as just another workplace environment.

'We run our clinics, of course, with state-of-the-art facilities. Along with more holistic therapies and emergency facilities for the community en route to the main hospital.'

'It looks as though you have everything you need here. I don't see what I could possibly add to your set-up.' Harriet wasn't being humble. She was aware that an experienced orthopaedic surgeon would be sought-after in a private clinic. There simply wasn't enough professional incentive in it for her.

While she wanted to help every person she could, she suspected the more challenging patients would be found in city hospitals and that was where she thrived. It was satisfying to improve a patient's quality of life by relieving pain and improving their mobility. Those with more insight into the human psyche might suggest a link to the mother she'd never felt she'd truly helped, and needed to atone for her perceived failure as a daughter. It was just as well she tried not to dwell on those things she couldn't fix and concentrated on those she could. With one exception. While the surroundings of her patients might be different, she wouldn't trade the number of lives she could improve for a matter of comfort or cash.

'You're the best in your field, Harriet. We both know that. Waiting lists for surgery can be backlogged for years and most people come here because they can't face the pain for that extended amount of time.'

'Spit it out, Charles. I know you're building up to something.' It wasn't simply her sparkling personality and unborn child he was after, by the sound of it.

'You know me too well.'

'Once upon a time, perhaps, but I don't presume to predict what's going on in your head any more.' The barb successfully managed to wipe the grin from his face and suggested she could still wound him. Although that wasn't going to achieve anything except make it harder for them to work alongside each other if she kept dragging up past hurt. If she ever entertained the idea of moving.

'The main reason for my visit today, and for bringing you with me, was to meet a few people.' He stopped looking at her as though she'd shot him in the chest and started up the huge marble staircase.

'Who?' Her borrowed boots were squeaking as she hurried to catch up with him down the corridor. She might be dressed appropriately for the Scottish winter climate, or Esme's place of work, but compared to Charles and the clinic she was out of place and under-dressed.

A city slicker transported into the birthplace of nobility, she could do without him trailing her around like a pet. She preferred to be the one in control of the facts and her daily schedule. Something she'd sworn she wouldn't give up for Charles or anyone else. Not even her firstborn.

Flora, the physiotherapist, was leaving the room they'd stopped at. 'Oh, hi. He seems to be moving a little better today. I'm sure he'll be glad to see you.'

'Thanks, Flora. We're just popping in to say hello.' He knocked on the door and waited for the resident inside to permit him entry. It was a simple gesture but showed the respect he had for his patients' privacy, treating them more as house guests than customers.

'Come…in.' A laboured male voice came from the other side of the door.

'I'm taking you in to see Gerry. He's recovering here after his stroke, so we're still working on getting his speech and mobility back on track.'

Harriet appreciated the heads up before they went in. A stroke could occur when a blockage prevented the blood supply reaching the brain, or because of a burst blood vessel. The resulting injury to the brain caused by a stroke could cause widespread and long-lasting problems. Including communication or irrational behaviour, caused by the psychological and cognitive impact of a stroke. It was always best to be prepared for such circumstances in case a patient became angry or resentful towards those trying to help them. Thankfully, such behaviour lessened as rehabilitation and recovery progressed.

The elderly gentleman was sitting in an armchair by the bed, clad in blue cotton pyjamas and trying his best to run a comb through his thinning white hair with a shaky hand.

'Hello, Mr Moore. I hope you don't mind me bringing a colleague of mine in to see you. This is Harriet.' Charles made the introduction and Harriet stepped forward to say hello.

'Call…me… Gerry. Lovely…to…meet… you… Harriet.'

His speech was slow and slurred. The evidence of his stroke was visible where the left side of his face drooped, but he still had a twinkle in his eye that said he had a lot of life still to live.

'You too, Gerry.' She took his hand and gently clasped it between both of hers.

'How is it going with Flora, your physiotherapist?' Charles sat on the edge of the bed, giving more of an impression that he was a visitor than the attending doctor.

'Task…master.' Gerry grinned.

'You certainly seem to be improving.' He nodded towards the comb, which was now balancing precariously on the edge of the nightstand. Harriet knew how important physio was to stroke patients to improve muscle strength with exercises. Although recovery could be slow, these small goals, such as picking up objects, were important. They encouraged patients on towards longer-term, more demanding goals such as standing or walking. It was all working towards getting the person's life back where possible.

'Can…feed…myself…now.'

'That's fantastic. I'll see if it's possible to have your meals with the other residents. The company will do you good.'

Gerry smiled at that but even the effort of speaking was obviously already taking its toll on him.

'We should get on and let you practise the exercises Flora has given you. I just wanted to call in and see how you were. I know the team are working with you but if you need to talk to me about how you're feeling, just let me know. This can be a confusing, frustrating time and I'm here, along with everyone else, to help you through this. The same goes for your wife. This is a lot for her to deal with too.' Charles shook his hand and Harriet said her goodbyes too. By the time they reached the door Gerry had already closed his eyes.

It was clear Charles went above and beyond the call of duty for his patients and if he was doing this to prove to her he was a nice guy at heart…well, it was working.

'He's a lovely man and he certainly seems to be recovering well.'

'I think it helps to have a multi-disciplinary team all under one roof. There are a lot of us working together in cases like this. You know orthopaedics could be used in conjunction with physiotherapy to work towards the best recovery. Surgery could provide stability to increase function in some instances.' Charles didn't have to convince her of the benefits of having a skilled team tailored to the needs of individual patients. She'd witnessed it for herself on occasion. The problem for her in joining the team at Heatherglen lay closer to home.

'Uh-huh?' She didn't give him the satisfaction of agreeing with him, but she was enjoying having him try to convince her. It gave her an insight into the work he was doing here, and the sort of man he'd become in her absence. A noble, conscientious one who only wanted the best for Heatherglen and his patients.

'I have someone else I'd like you to meet. If you want to?' He hesitated, perhaps picking up on her wariness about getting drawn into this.

'Of course.' She didn't want him to think she wasn't interested in his work when that was supposed to be the reason behind this visit.

He led her down the hall to another room and knocked on the door. A cheery, young voice shouted for him to come in.

Charles opened the door and ushered Harriet into the room. 'This is the Dawson family. Everyone, this is Harriet Bell, a friend who's staying with us at Heatherglen.'

'Hi.' The young girl in the bed could only have been about seven or eight with her parents sitting close by. Her adorable gap-toothed smile stole anyone's right to be in a bad mood when she was the one hooked up to hospital machinery.

'Bryony is my favourite patient but don't tell anyone else in case they get jealous.' Charles winked at the little girl, who giggled in response. He was charming a child as easily as he had her when they'd first met. It gave some indication of what an excellent father he would make. One more reason to like him she didn't need.

'Hello, Bryony.' Harriet greeted Mr and Mrs Dawson too, though she didn't know why Charles had brought her here.

'Is Harriet your girlfriend?' Bryony asked. The Charles-crushing apparently started from an early age.

Harriet found herself watching and waiting for his reply as intensely as his little admirer. Ridiculous when she hadn't held that title for a considerable part of her adult life.

'I told you, Ms Bell is a surgeon, like me. Except she works with people's bones instead of their noggins.' He rapped his knuckles on his skull and set off more childish laughter, successfully avoiding answering the personal question.

'Can you fix my legs?' With the directness only a child could get away with, Bryony challenged Harriet directly.

'I'm sorry, I...er...' Put on the spot, she felt compelled to answer without knowing anything of Bryony's medical history, or how long her connection to Heatherglen as a medical practitioner would last.

'Harriet's just visiting but I'd like to share your details with her, if that's okay?' He was checking with Bryony as much as her parents but all three nodded their consent.

Harriet had the ominous feeling of having walked into a trap.

'Bryony has cerebral palsy. At the minute she has a baclofen pump to help with the chronic pain. It's a small device implanted in her abdomen connected to the spinal cord by a thin tube under her skin. It continuously dispenses medication through the spinal column and delivers muscle relaxant to reduce tightness.' Undergoing surgery at such a young age made the children more special to the medical staff involved. There were always risks and no one undertook these procedures lightly on such fragile bodies. Bryony certainly seemed to have a special place in Charles's heart.

As an orthopaedic surgeon she had a lot of experience with CP too. Cerebral palsy— a group of conditions caused by an issue with the brain around the time of birth— led to difficulties with muscle strength and movement. The severity of the condition varied from patient to patient, but many came to her to address problems of muscle spasticity and contractures. With surgery, Harriet was able to help release muscles that were too tight or transfer strong muscles for weak ones. In some cases, she operated on the joints themselves, to aid deformity preventing basic motor function.

All of which Charles would've known before bringing her in here. However, the history of the patient's condition and potential for improvement had to be taken into consideration before surgery. She couldn't volunteer her skills without extensive consultation with a team of carers and specialists to set realistic goals. Something she was willing to do if asked.

'I hope the pump helps you feel better soon.' Although she didn't want to reference it for fear of upsetting the family, Harriet was aware it must've been hard to have gone through this, especially over Christmas.

'Recovery has taken longer than expected. Bryony picked up a virus from her little brother right after surgery, but we hope to have you home soon, don't we?' Charles obviously had been thinking the same thing and Harriet would've been surprised if he hadn't paid a visit at some point yesterday, as he was so fond of her.

'Santa sent me a letter to say he'll make a special stop at my house when I'm better.'

'Because you're such a brave and special girl.' Her mum rested a hand on her daughter's forehead, but Harriet didn't miss the glances exchanged between her and Charles.

She got the impression he might've had a hand in that letter. In fact, she'd go as far to say it was probably in his handwriting.

'We're going to have a second special Christmas once Bryony's home.' As Bryony disclosed the contents of her extensive, unicorn-themed Christmas list, her mother looked as though she'd enjoy it as much as her daughter, knowing she'd be home safe.

A sudden jolt of awareness at the role she was about to take on almost knocked Harriet off her feet. Every decision she made from now on, every emotion was going to be tied to this baby. Just as Mrs Dawson's happiness and peace of mind were centred around her child. It didn't matter what happened between her and Charles, Scotland and London, this baby's welfare came first.

Her hand automatically rested on her stomach, already protecting him or her. The movement didn't escape Charles's notice as his gaze followed the action.

'Bryony's suffering twenty percent spasticity in her limbs. She was mobile, but the pain has become too much for her lately. There's no guarantee on how long the pump will last, so that means another operation further down the road.' Charles shared that extra difficult news out of Bryony's earshot.

Harriet's heart broke a fraction more for the family she'd become attached to in such a short space of time. If it was her child she'd want everything humanly possible done to stop her hurting.

'How can I help?' she asked, knowing she'd committed to coming back to Heatherglen.

CHAPTER FIVE

CHARLES HADN'T BROUGHT Harriet here to guilt her into assisting him with Bryony's treatment. He would've been here regardless of his ex's presence, but he wouldn't apologise for wanting Harriet to see the difference she could make at Heatherglen. The little girl had had a tough time of it as had her parents, and he would do everything in his power to make things easier for them.

When he had the ear of an orthopaedic surgeon with Harriet's experience it made sense to get her advice. It was simply a bonus on a personal level if she got involved and maintained an interest that saw her return, or stay for good.

'I'm going to show Harriet around the rest of the clinic, but I'll be back to see you all later.' He shook hands with Bryony's parents, who knew he couldn't spend all day at their daughter's bedside when they had other children at home on a post-Santa high. But he'd do his best to call in and provide some company for Bryony when he could. He knew Harriet well enough to expect her to want to do the same. Perhaps spending quality time with a child would show her what could be gained by sharing parenting responsibility. She could easily walk away, deny him any access to the child she was carrying, after the way he'd treated her in the past, but he wanted her to see they'd be better as a team. That their baby would be better off here, with both parents. A family.

The triumphant smile he was wearing as Harriet was saying her goodbyes to the family died on his lips. A wagging, panting bundle of fur streaked past him as he opened the door to leave the room.

'What the—?'

'Isn't this Esme's puppy?' Harriet scooped up the excitable animal, which had been causing havoc recently.

'He's so sweet. Is he for me?' Bryony's voice matched the excitement of the canine intruder and he cursed his sister's generous heart. If Esme hadn't insisted on keeping this nuisance around, he wouldn't have to upset a young patient.

'Sorry, Bryony. He must've escaped from the house.'

'You can stroke him if you want.' Harriet stepped in with a compromise and took the dog over to her before the tears had an opportunity to fully form.

'He tickles.' Bryony giggled as Dougal licked her face. Charles wasn't pleased that Dougal had made an unscheduled, unsupervised visit but it was good to see her happy. Harriet too. Although the dogs were part of the ongoing therapy around here, he'd still have to have a word with Esme about keeping a closer eye on her four-legged friend. He didn't want Dougal getting in the way when staff were doing their rounds.

He lifted the hand sanitiser and passed it to her mother. 'I'm so sorry about this.'

'Don't worry. He's the best therapy we could have asked for.' Bryony's mother joined the group fawning over Dougal as though he were a newborn baby. Now, that kind of interest he could understand. When their child was born he'd expect the whole world to take notice. But a dog?

He understood their importance in terms of therapy here. He'd seen the results for himself. They calmed patients as well as providing a distraction from illness and treatment. However, on a personal level he didn't know what the fuss was about. He'd never been a dog lover. Probably because his parents had stressed how much mess and destruction they could cause in a place like this where every stick of furniture had historic and monetary value. As proved by their canine companion. Sure, Dougal was cute, but he didn't do anything for Charles except generally make his life more difficult around here.

'We should get him back where he's supposed to be.' Charles stood back and let Harriet and her new friend leave before him.

''Bye, Dougal.' There was a chorus as they left, indicating there was only one of them who'd be truly missed.

'Just wait until I see Esme. I'd prefer he

had a bath at least before he starts wandering around the place.'

'Oh, poor baby, don't listen to the nasty man. You smell like home to me.' Harriet covered Dougal's ears against the insult and peppered him with kisses, completely losing her own professional image to let her soft-hearted mothering instinct take over.

'You lived in a kennel?'

She tutted. 'We always had a dog in the house when I was growing up with Mum. They're great company and totally devoted to their owners. If I wasn't so busy with work, I'd still have one, but it wouldn't be fair to leave one at home alone all day.'

'Exactly why he shouldn't be in the castle, unsupervised, while Esme is at work.'

Harriet had talked about her parents and how difficult her childhood had been, with an absent father and an over-dependent mother, but she'd never mentioned having pets. She took so much joy from being around Dougal, a picture of their little family, complete with raucous pets, flashed into his head and suddenly he didn't mind at all.

'He's only a baby. Esme is the expert and

she only has his best interests at heart. How could you be mad at this little face?' She held Dougal out towards him. The dog's tail was wagging so hard his body nearly folded in two.

Charles stared into the pair of soulful eyes begging for his love. A little pink doggie tongue shot out and began slobbering over his face, making it impossible to remember why he was being a grouch.

Then a warm trickle of liquid soaked through his suit and reminded him.

'Dougal!'

'Whoops. I think he got too excited.' Harriet could barely contain her laughter as the puppy promptly forgot all the house training Esme had no doubt instilled in him.

Harriet didn't know how Charles was going to react to a little pee as she laughed at his expense. It was understandable he would be upset at the dog running amok in the clinic but there'd been no real harm done, other than to his suit.

Charles rolled his eyes, took the pup from

her, and held him at arm's length as he headed towards the front door.

'You can't abandon him outside. It's too cold.' Even with his jaunty Christmas jumper he'd freeze to death out there. She wouldn't stand back and let that happen. She'd never forgive herself and Esme would never forgive either of them.

'What do you take me for, Harriet? I'm not a complete monster.' Her accusation stopped Charles in his snow-covered tracks. It highlighted how much work was required on her trust issues with him before the baby arrived.

She didn't dispute his intentions were honourable in his desire for them to raise the child here, at least in his eyes, but sometimes that wasn't enough. This time she'd need more than promises to persuade her to change her life for him.

After all, this was only a helpless pup and a baby was going to cause much more disruption. She would do whatever it took for her child to have a stable home life and history had shown Charles couldn't always be counted on.

Nevertheless, she followed him to the canine therapy centre and was blown away by the changes there too. The old stables had been modernised with huge windows, opening the building up to welcome people inside. A huge investment of time, money and love had gone into the clinic and the centre. A commitment Charles hadn't managed to make to her.

'I'm sorry. You didn't seem very sympathetic to him.' If he couldn't put up with Esme mollycoddling an abandoned pooch in her own home, it didn't seem so far-fetched to think he'd chuck it out in the snow.

'The dogs are a great asset here but they're Esme's responsibility. I don't want to spend my days chasing after them when I'm trying to work. It's my job to make sure the patients are comfortable during their treatment and Esme's to train the dogs. I'm sympathetic to a point but I can't have puppies running amok in the clinic. As well as the professional issue I have with what happened today, I guess I'm just not a doggie person. We were never encouraged to have pets in the castle because of the potential mess and damage they could cause and that has stuck with me. That doesn't mean I'm incapable of showing love and compassion to a baby. Despite whatever is going on in that head of yours.'

It sounded so ridiculous out loud she blushed. Charles was justifiably upset by the accusation. She'd overreacted. This was the real reason she'd agreed to spend time here—to find out who he really was now and decide if this was the right environment to raise their child after all. If his ego took a bashing in the process he'd simply have to get over it. As a father-to-be he was going to have to put the needs of the baby above his pride.

'Charles! Harriet! It's nice of you to stop by.'

'I believe this is yours.' Charles presented Esme with the canine criminal who didn't look the least bit guilty as he licked her face.

'What are you doing out here, mister?' Esme nuzzled her face into the bundle and Harriet wondered how the siblings could interact so differently with the animal.

'Good question. You can pay the dry-cleaning bill for my suit.' Charles arched an eyebrow at them both.

'Oh, dear. He didn't, did he? Dougal loves you, that's why he gets so excited to see you.' She too was doing little to hide the laughter at her brother's misfortune.

'Yeah, well, the feeling is definitely not mutual. You're going to have to increase his security detail.'

'He's not some sort of criminal mastermind. He probably slipped out through the door when you weren't looking.' Esme inadvertently tripped Harriet's guilt switch. It was possible she hadn't been paying close attention to anything other than Charles's sunny disposition when they'd left this morning. It seemed such a long time ago now.

'It might be my fault. I think I was the last one out this morning.' She confessed her misdemeanour, glad something more serious hadn't happened if it had been her who'd left the door ajar.

'It's not your fault.' Charles was quick to absolve her of responsibility, though he'd been keen to hold Esme to account for the same incident.

'It's no one's fault. What my brother has neglected to tell you is that this isn't the first time this has happened. As much as I've tried to partner Dougal with Max, he prefers Charles's company. The dog, not Max.'

'Goodness knows why.' Charles brushed off the idea, but Harriet had witnessed the puppy's love for herself.

'We should've called him Houdini. It doesn't matter where we put him, he always manages to escape and track down his favourite person in the whole world.'

'I wish he wouldn't.'

'You're fighting a losing battle, dear brother. Just give in and accept you're the leader of Dougal's pack.'

'Never.' Despite his refusal the scowl had broken on Charles's face, hinting that he wasn't as immune to the cute little mongrel as he made out. It was nicer to imagine him sitting in his armchair with a dog curled up contentedly in his lap than a man capable of leaving a puppy out in the snow. Then it wasn't such a stretch to picture him cooing over a baby.

'He certainly made an impression on Bryony, the young patient whose room he barged into.' Harriet attempted to shift her thoughts to someone who wasn't a part of her soon-to-be family. She wanted to remain objective where a potential work environment was concerned and keep her confused feelings about Charles out of any career decision. He'd taken the last one out of her hands and now she wanted control of the next. Minus his influence.

Esme grimaced as she heard about Dougal's exploits. 'I'm so sorry. Max and I have been checking on him regularly. I don't want to have to lock him into a dog crate. It's important he gets used to a home environment.'

'Preferably without wrecking it in the process,' Charles added.

'Charles and I can take him with us and keep an eye on him until you've finished here. We'll have to go back anyway.' Harriet indicated the ruined suit, which wasn't going to do anything to improve his attitude towards Dougal with the constant reminder of his humiliation.

'Would you? That would be so helpful. I have my hands full here.' Esme passed the pooch parcel again as a dozen others sounded their demands for her attention.

'You owe me one, sis.' Even Charles seemed to realise her workload could do without one more demanding dog as he accepted his fate of puppy-sitting for the rest of the afternoon.

Harriet feared for Dougal's future if he got on Charles's bad side again or damaged more than the Laird's cool façade.

'Excuse me if I'm speaking out of turn, but there was one positive to come out of this mishap.' All eyes were on Harriet now, including Dougal's, begging her to save him from eviction.

'I'm dying to hear this.' Charles folded his arms and waited for the defence.

She ignored the cynicism and the childish urge to stick her tongue out at him. 'Bryony, Charles's patient with cerebral palsy responded well to Dougal and I know you train therapy dogs here. Is there a chance you could partner the two together?' It would solve the immediate problem by finding Dougal alternative accommodation and at the same time provide the young girl with a much-needed companion.'

Charles was so busy laughing it was left to Esme to explain the flaw in that plan. 'Unfortunately, I'm not sure Dougal is going to be suitable for training. Not unless we use Charles as an incentive. We can look into alternatives for Bryony if the family is interested. We train a lot of dogs to help cerebral palsy patients. They seem to get a lot out of having therapy dogs.'

Harriet nodded. She understood the joy of having unconditional love from a pet during tough times. A dog could only aid Bryony through the challenges she endured.

'I can mention it to her parents and get them to come and talk it over with you if they're interested.' Now they were on the subject of his patient Charles resumed his professional manner and took the suggestion seriously. Although it didn't help with the Dougal problem, Harriet was satisfied her idea hadn't been as ridiculous as she'd initially feared.

'Great. I can give them a tour and put them in touch with some of our other CP families.' Esme gave her brother a swift kiss on the cheek and did the same to Harriet before disappearing back into the kennels, leaving Harriet and Charles to mind her fur baby.

'Stay!' Everyone in the vicinity could've told him it was a pointless command by now, but Charles attempted to assert his authority all the same.

Dougal had that same goofball expression, tongue hanging out the side of his mouth, tail wagging, with no intention of doing anything he was told. Charles had no idea why he was so irresistible when there was a bowl of dog food and a comfy bed waiting nearby. He knew where he'd rather be. Especially when there were belly rubs and Harriet kisses on offer elsewhere.

Naturally, the little mongrel had made a run for it the second Charles turned his back and it was only Harriet's quick reflexes that had saved him from further dog slobber.

'I'll keep him company while you get changed,' she promised, burying her face in Dougal's fur.

'If you wouldn't mind, I think I'll grab a quick shower.' A cold one. Then he might burn his Dougal-scented suit.

'Go. I'll be happy to get some snuggles without you scowling at us.' He thought she was joking but he and the mischievous pup were going to have to get along if he was going to impress Harriet. Besides, if Esme had anything to do with it, Dougal was going to be a long-term resident. Charles was simply going to have to get used to changes around here.

Some breathing space between him and Harriet was good, he realised, casting off his clothes to step into the shower. He'd jumped in with that offer to Harriet to join them at the clinic on the basis he'd be closer to the baby. However, the more time he spent with Harriet the more he could see what he'd given up twelve years ago.

If that one night in bed had reminded him

what they'd had together physically—and, boy, it had improved with age—being in her company today had brought out that caring side he'd admired so much in her. She was good at her job, that had never been in doubt, but it was her extra interest in Bryony, and that stupid dog, that took him back to the reasons he'd fallen for her in the first place.

It was a shame she'd made it clear she didn't trust him to commit to more than one night together. He didn't blame her but the reasons for wanting her to stay at Heatherglen were becoming more personal by the second.

He wanted to have it all—a successful career, a memorial honouring his brother and father, and a family of his own, including a partner to share it all with. Yet he knew it was selfish. Something that always spelled disaster for those closest to him. The ones he was supposed to love.

He was pushing her to transfer to Cluchlochry for the baby's sake because *he* wanted her to. Really, what was in it for her? There were better career prospects in London and that was the reason he'd sacrificed a life with her in the first place. It wasn't fair to pressure her. Hopefully they could resolve this with a proper conversation about what was best for all of them. It wasn't the first time he'd had to rein in his feelings for her and he'd survived. They both had.

Once the water had turned colder than he was prepared to subject himself to, he stepped out of the shower and wrapped a towel around his waist.

The en suite bathroom made his wardrobe accessible without having to compromise his modesty.

If he was spending the afternoon with Sir Pees-a-Lot, he wasn't going to risk another good suit. He bypassed the smart shirts and trousers, reaching for the comfy, less expensive option of a well-worn pair of jeans and a sweater.

The bedroom door burst open just as he was about to unfasten the towel. A flash of brindle brown, a tug at the hem of the towel and Charles felt cold air on his naked skin.

He exclaimed in exasperation, 'What the hell…?'

That was closely followed by Harriet's
'Dougal!'

As she ran into the room Charles was
left cupping his hands over his privates to
save both their blushes. Nothing she hadn't
seen before but the way she was staring at
him made him feel more exposed than ever.
He should've been flattered by the blatant
ogling but with a rogue puppy wrestling
with his towel on his bedroom floor it was
downright embarrassing.

'Well, this is awkward.' He sidestepped
towards the clothes he had laid out on his
bed, wondering how he could dress without
flashing her again.

Harriet blinked at him a few times before
she became animated again. 'Oh, my goodness. I'm so sorry, Charles. He slipped past
me when I was putting the kettle on for a cup
of tea. He's as fast as lightning.'

'It's okay. You need eyes in the back of
your head to watch this one.' What else
could he say to make this whole episode less
embarrassing for both of them? This dog had
a lot to answer for.

'Dougal. Drop it. Drop it.' Harriet attempted to retrieve the towel Charles would appreciate having back. Dougal clamped on tighter to his prize. Charles knew at first hand those little teeth were like needles.

'Leave it. If the two of you wouldn't mind leaving, I might salvage some of my dignity.' An unfortunate choice of words given what he was clutching at the moment.

'No problem. Sorry. Again.' She reached for the dignity-destroyer, who saw this as some sort of game and dashed away every time Harriet came close. Eventually she managed to grab one end of the towel and entered into a tug of war.

It was all becoming ridiculous now. All they needed was Esme to walk in on this farce and she'd laugh herself into a coma.

'Give. Me. The. Damn. Towel.' Harriet gave one last yank and emerged victorious, clutching the now chewed towel. Although she did manage to land flat on her backside in the process. Dougal had bested them both.

'I'm not sure who won that one. I'd help you up but…' He shrugged, unable to come out of this situation as a gentleman.

She stood up and held the towel out to

him. Even then he wasn't sure how to accept it without making another show of himself.

'You might want to close your eyes or something.'

'Don't be silly. We're both adults.' The twinkle in her eyes said she wasn't offended, or surprised, by what she'd seen.

She wrapped the towel around his waist for him, pressing her body to his as she did so. Close enough that Charles could hear the hitch in her breath, feel her warmth on his skin, and it was torture that he couldn't do a thing about it.

Harriet sensed his eyes on her before she saw him watching her so intently. So much for remaining emotionally detached. Now here she was standing in his bedroom with her arms wrapped around Charles's lower half with the most recent image of what lay beneath burned on her brain.

Her skin was flushed with the heat of arousal, not embarrassment, remembering the last time she'd had her hands on his naked body. It would be easy to fall into bed with him again and forget everything except how good he could make her feel.

'Harriet…' That husky tone of his desire shot straight to her loins, cutting off all common sense in favour of a more basic need.

She closed her eyes against temptation, but it didn't help her forget the softness of his lips, the memory of him kissing her fresh enough to make hers tingle.

'Don't.' It was a plea for him to stop. If he made a move on her she couldn't resist because she didn't want to. She ached for him and to share his bed again. It was only her long-held insecurities maintaining that last defence.

Sex with Charles would only complicate her life. London had proved that. Her seduction hadn't given her any sort of closure but instead had opened a whole new chapter between them.

He rested his chin on her head and sighed. A reflection of Harriet's own frustration at their situation. She wanted to cry but Charles continued to hold her as though he was drawing as much comfort as she was from this embrace.

Yes, he was wearing virtually nothing, and she was aware of every taut inch of him as she pressed her cheek against his chest. Even if he'd been fully clothed in a room full of people the moment would've been as touching, and intimate.

They'd made mistakes and suffered as a result, but they couldn't go back and change anything any more than they could predict what was going to happen. She couldn't remember the last time someone had simply held her, or when she'd let them. Accepting comfort seemed like a failure to her. As though the stresses of life had defeated her. She'd learned long ago not to give in and admit she couldn't do everything on her own. Growing up with her mother hadn't left room for two to wallow in personal hardship. One of them had to be strong enough to carry the other and in her case, the child had become the parent.

Later, when Charles had broken her heart, she'd been in need of a shoulder to cry on. With none available she'd soldiered on lest she let melancholy consume her as it had her mother. Since then, she'd cultivated pride in her independence and in taking back control of her emotions.

This warmth from his touch even without the physical attraction reminded her of everything she'd been missing in her pursuit of a self-sufficient life.

She sighed, and Charles continued to maintain the simple contact. Given their traumatic history and the break-up he'd told her he hadn't wanted, it was possible he'd been living in emotional isolation too. Even though he mightn't have replaced her in his affections, the thought didn't please her. Rather, sadness settled over her as she realised what they'd both lost.

A sharp yelp reminded them Dougal was in the room and they broke apart.

'I think someone wants your attention.' Charles was smiling at her, but his hangdog expression was tugging at her heartstrings more than the little one nipping at her heel. The fact Charles might crave something more than her attention was something she couldn't afford to indulge.

'He's due a feed.'

'I can see that,' Charles laughed as Dougal

caught the bottom of his towel and tugged again. This time Charles was ready and managed to keep a tight hold of his modesty.

'This time I'll lock him in solitary confinement if I have to.' The dog was turning out to be such an excellent guardian against her making bad decisions she might just adopt him herself.

CHAPTER SIX

'IT'S MY WAY of saying thank you for not driving Dougal to the nearest dog pound.'

Esme plated up the dinner she'd insisted on cooking, regardless that she'd only recently finished work. She was another one who didn't submit to a typical nine-to-five schedule but had made an effort to get home to cook this feast.

'Really, you didn't have to.'

Harriet would have settled for something as plain as a slice of toast. Her stomach had been somersaulting since she'd walked into Charles's room to find him naked. The sight of him sitting opposite her at the dinner table in his casual wear hadn't lessened the impact he'd had on her when she'd set eyes on him again.

Now, as well as the memories of rolling

around in bed with him, his very presence reminded her of the vulnerability of being in his arms. When she'd let go of everything except the bliss she'd found in his embrace. It was unnerving that she'd lost that much control around him, yet she yearned to do it again and again. It didn't help when the four of them—Esme, Charles, Max and herself—seemed like they were on a double date. At worst, a family meal she was intruding on or anything else she didn't have a legitimate reason to attend.

Charles tucked into the home-cooked meal with gusto, his appetite greater than Harriet's.

'This is amazing.' Max reached across to squeeze Esme's hand in thanks and the pure love in their eyes for each other was so touching Harriet had to turn away before she started blubbing.

It was hard to believe she and Charles had ever been that oblivious to the world around them, though they must've been at some point. Certainly, Charles had blamed their relationship for making him blind to his father's struggles after Nick had died. That was what had made his blunt dismissal so hard to accept when she'd still been loved up. If Max turned on Esme now it would blindside her too, Harriet was sure. Love was a painful business.

'So, what did you guys get up to this afternoon after you left the centre?' As innocent as it was, Esme's question almost made Harriet choke on her dinner as a naked Charles sprang to mind.

He was smirking at her now, daring her to share their adventures in his bedroom, which, although without serious incident, were memorable all the same. It turned out to be something she'd prefer to keep private between them for more than one reason.

'We were…er…busy trying to keep Dougal out of trouble.' Eventually Charles jumped in with a truthful half-answer.

Harriet couldn't help but smile at him in thanks and because of the memories of the pup running rings around them.

'He'll be out of your hair tomorrow. Max is going to install safety gates. You know, the ones you use for babies. They'll come in handy in the future anyway.' It was at the last second Esme caught what she was saying. Max too, judging by the expression of horror on his face.

'Harriet's pregnant,' Esme blurted out, probably before Max keeled over thinking she was the one planning a baby in the near future.

Charles dropped his knife and fork onto his plate with a clatter. 'For goodness' sake. Harriet asked you to keep it yourself.'

'Sorry,' Esme mumbled into her chest, but Harriet would've been surprised if she hadn't shared the news with Max at some point, given the close nature of their relationship.

'It's fine. Don't worry. We've just found out we're expecting, Max, and we're trying to figure things out at the moment.' She didn't know how much of their history he was aware of but there was no reason to make anyone feel guilty about the situation. The news had to come out some time.

Max nodded sagely. 'Sure. It's a lot to take in. I won't breathe a word to anyone.'

'Thanks.' For all Harriet knew, she'd be gone by the end of the week, with no need to put Max or Esme under pressure to keep their secret.

'Congratulations.' Max raised a glass to toast them and Harriet clinked her water against it.

'You too, mate.' He reached across the table to shake Charles's hand.

'Cheers.' Charles was beaming, and the simple acceptance of the unplanned pregnancy began to make her feel part of the family. Not the best environment to nurture that sense of isolation she needed to maintain control in her life.

Heatherglen was offering that support to her child she hadn't had growing up, but she wasn't convinced it would be a good move for her personally. A miserable mother, as she knew, did not a happy childhood make. It would take her to get past her feelings about Charles, positive and negative, to be able to face him on a daily basis.

'Harriet and I are going to take a trip into the village tomorrow.' Charles dropped the next bombshell into the middle of their meal.

'We are?'

'You are?' Esme echoed Harriet's surprise

at the announcement when he hadn't con-sulted either of them.

He carried on eating without missing a beat. 'I thought I could show you around. The shops should be open again and I expect you'll need to get a few things.'

'I do.' The trip would take them away from the patients, family and four-legged friends who'd provided a necessary buffer between them today, leaving them alone. A danger-ous position as this afternoon had demon-strated. Yet the gesture proved he had been thinking about her, about spending time with her, and anticipating her needs for her unex-pected extended stay. She couldn't turn him down even if she wanted to.

Out of the corner of her eye Harriet could see Esme shaking her head.

'What?' Charles demanded to know why she disapproved of his plan. Harriet too won-dered why such a thoughtful gesture should warrant the negative response.

'You never take time off. Yesterday was Christmas Day and you spent most of it at the clinic. It's so unlike you, bro.'

He shrugged. 'Maybe I have different priorities now.'

Harriet snapped her head up at that.

'Already? Wow. Fatherhood must be agreeing with you.' His sister teased him, their back and forth relationship dizzying, but it showed how close they were. Only two people who loved each other could generate such strong and varying degrees of emotion. One minute they were at each other's throats, gently joshing the next. If Harriet had had a sibling, she would've had someone on her side supporting her through the ups and downs. She might not have shut down emotionally over the years if she'd had someone giving her a kick up the backside when she'd required it. Annoying her when she hadn't.

It was a nice idea that her little one might have that family support but it made her consider what sort of relationship she had with Charles. Their lives had already been turned upside down without future family planning too. They weren't even together. In case she'd forgotten it, she was supposed to be putting him off the idea of her hanging around so she could return to London. It was ridiculous to go down the road of believing they could have a family together when their circumstances were so unstable.

Yet he was making an effort to convince her and Esme he was going to change and manage his time at Heatherglen so he could devote himself to her and the baby. This wasn't the Charles she'd anticipated finding at the castle, Laird of all he surveyed and unwilling to give up anything for anyone. Now every little thing he did for her, every concession was going to make it harder for her to walk away when the time came.

'Ready?' Charles waited for her to belt herself in, his hand on the ignition key as though he was giving her the opportunity to bale out. This venture was about more than replenishing her wardrobe. He was showing her he would prioritise her when he had to. The significance wasn't lost on Harriet, but anyone could make a promise. It was being true to your word that counted. Only with time and a history of seeing things through could she be convinced he meant what he said.

She couldn't expect Charles to drop work to take her on a shopping jaunt when the mood struck, neither would she want him to. It wasn't the commitment to his patients she had an issue with. Raising a child necessitated making small compromises on a regular basis for school runs, holidays or illness. Children didn't run to a schedule and Harriet would rather manage it all on her own than have him complain every time he had to make alternative work arrangements.

'As ready as I'll ever be,' she sighed, and buckled up for the bumpy ride they were about to undertake.

'The roads have turned icy overnight so I'll take it easy. I'm carrying a precious load after all.'

She didn't know if he was talking about her or the baby as he negotiated the frosty lanes with his foot hovering on the brake. They came as a package now but that would change, physically, in about seven months' time.

If she decided not to move and he wanted their child at weekends and holidays it was going to be difficult. Should she have other work commitments, or Charles no longer thought of her as part of the equation, the separation was bound to be stressful. She was already fitting in here way too easily, with everyone being so accommodating. In some ways it was like being a child again, only with people who were taking her feelings into consideration along with their own.

'It's like a scene from a Christmas film where they've thrown in every cliché they could think of to make it look festive here.' In the city, snow was a cold, slushy nuisance, causing accidents and slowing traffic to a standstill. Here in the country she was able to take the time to appreciate the beauty in the weather. The white undisturbed fields, glistening invitingly, made Harriet want to roll around and make her mark where no one else had.

As they approached the village, the cosy fairy-tale cottages coughed wisps of smoke into the freezing air and told of the families inside sitting around the fire.

'Different from London?' Charles would take this vista for granted when he had it on his doorstep. Gaudy lights, over-decorated trees and throngs of harassed shoppers would be as much of a novelty to him as this was to her. It was only the potential hazards of the season that linked the vastly different locations.

They stopped at a junction just outside the village to check for oncoming traffic, only for the car to continue travelling out onto the road after Charles had applied the handbrake.

'We must've hit a patch of black ice.' Very experienced in driving in these kinds of conditions, he did his best to control the vehicle, steering into the skid instead of fighting against it.

The car eventually slid to a halt and Harriet sent fervent thanks to the heavens that they were alone on the road. They would've been helpless should anyone else have been coming towards them. Instinctively she wrapped her arms around her belly, that mama bear already fully formed and protective of her cub.

'Are you all right?' Another hand covered hers.

'No harm done,' she assured him, but it

was apparent papa bear was making himself known too.

'I'll take a different route back. It's longer but the roads might be gritted out that way.'

Harriet muttered agreeable sounds as shock began to set in about what could have happened. At that second she realised her baby's life was more precious to her than her own. She'd give up anything to ensure this child was safe. Including her job and her house if she was sure Heatherglen would be the best place to provide security.

It took several attempts to get the car going in the direction they wanted. That was mainly because Charles refused to let her get out and lighten the weight of the car. The result of spinning tyres as he attempted to get traction on the slick surface was the smell of burning rubber.

The spinning motion of the vehicle combined with the acrid air had her clutching her belly now for a different reason.

'I have to get out, Charles.' It was a warning for him to pull over before his car was filled with more than fumes.

'What is it? What's wrong?' He immediately pulled over to the grass verge.

'Air,' she gasped, nausea rising too fast for her to quell with willpower alone.

Charles unbuckled his seat belt and jumped out of the car before she could stop him. He slipped and slid around the side of the car in his hurry to get to her. 'Be careful. We don't want any more accidents.'

With one hand steady on the now open passenger door, he held the other out to her.

'I just need some fresh air. There's no panic.' Embarrassed by the sudden bout of nausea, she ignored the helping hand to stand on her own two feet unassisted. A plan that went awry as soon as her foot slipped on the ice and she had to accept all the support offered.

'I've got you.' He caught her and braced her against the side of the car with his body.

She closed her eyes and wished the world would stop spinning. 'I'm fine.'

'Look at me. Open your eyes and focus on me, Harriet. That's it. Now, take deep breaths. In...and out.' Charles called her back from the brink of oblivion promising to take her somewhere safe.

She followed his instructions, inhaling his familiar scent, so reassuring and irresistible. Despite her return to full consciousness Charles kept a tight hold on her.

'Has this happened before?'

'No, but I don't usually spend my mornings doing doughnuts in the car.' Sarcasm was her only defence when she was at his mercy.

'I'd never have come if I'd realised the roads were so bad. Do you want to go home?' He eased her back into the passenger seat so she was sitting sideways with Charles kneeling at her feet.

His feelings of guilt were almost palpable, but revenge wasn't something she'd ever wanted in coming to Heatherglen.

'No. It's probably just shock, or morning sickness, or motion sickness. It'll pass.'

'You know it's not a weakness to be sick or, heaven forbid, to let someone help you.' He was holding both of her hands and Harriet could picture him in the delivery suite with her with the same calm presence, coaching her through labour. She hadn't re-alised how much she needed someone like that in her life so she could take a breather once in a while and let someone be strong for her.

However, the birth was a long way off and anything could happen in the interim. It wouldn't do to become reliant on Charles for support if he wasn't going to be there at the crucial time.

'Honestly, I feel a lot better. I'd rather get back on my feet and find something to distract me. Now, you said something about shops?' With steadier movements than before, she exited the car and slammed the door, forcing him to take a step back.

In London the shops would already be bulging at the seams with savvy shoppers seeking bargains in the sales. Cluchlochry was quiet, as though in hibernation, waiting for spring before the inhabitants would emerge back into the daylight.

Charles huffed out a cloud of breath into the atmosphere, but he'd stopped arguing with her. If these past couple of days had shown him anything about the woman she'd become, he'd realised she was much stronger than the one he'd known previously. Headstrong, stubborn, she'd heard it said before from other people whose interference in her life she'd refused to accept. It was that self-defence mechanism that had protected her fragile heart from any further sledgehammer blows. She had to keep that superwoman cape on at all times. Especially around Charles.

'Christmas is over. People have a living to make. I'm sure they'll be glad to see customers in their businesses and we can always stop for lunch at McKinney's pub.'

Harriet was curious about the shops, which were missing the garish signs the high-street stores usually displayed. If anything, the shopfronts here blended in too well with the surroundings. Especially now it had begun snowing again in earnest and limiting visibility.

'Any suggestions about where we should begin our shopping trip?' Left to her, she was afraid of walking in on some unsuspecting local watching TV in her parlour because she couldn't tell the business premises from the residential buildings.

'There's a wool shop if you fancy taking up knitting.'

'Why would I?' She rounded on him, waiting for the explanation, which was bound to begin a debate about stereotypical gender association.

'It's the sort of thing wo…people do when there's a baby on the way, isn't it?' Charles's face was unreadable as he waved at the proprietor standing by her colourful window display of yarn.

Harriet hoped he was joking.

'Are you honing your carpentry skills so you can knock a crib together, then?' It was a jibe to get back at him for insinuating she should be sitting knitting bootees for the duration of her 'confinement'.

Not one to give her the satisfaction of winning an argument, Charles countered with a chirpy, 'Maybe I will.'

Now she was going to be plagued with a sultry montage of him in her head, his naked torso beaded with sweat as he lovingly crafted a masterpiece with his rough, strong hands. Looking for a distraction from her over-active imagination, she pushed open the next shop door.

'Hello, there.' The shopkeeper didn't need the jingle of the bell to alert her that she had customers.

'Hi, Joanie. This is Harriet, a friend of the family. I'm just showing her around the village.' Charles made the introduction and Harriet wondered for the first time if any of the locals would remember the scandal of the young Laird's failed romance. The rumour mill would be working overtime if they heard she was back, pregnant.

'Nice to meet you, Joanie.' Harriet shook her hand, already getting friendly vibes from the pleasant redhead and her quirky shop.

The shelves were packed with all manner of knick-knacks and cute gifts tourists and children would lap up. Unfortunately, there was nothing in stock that would aid her quest for a bigger wardrobe.

'Your hands are freezing. Let me make you a cup of tea to warm you up.' Joanie wouldn't hear another word on the subject and disappeared into the back of the shop, ignoring any protest.

'Hot sugary tea is exactly what you need.' Charles pulled over a couple of chairs to the counter and gave the impression that impromptu tea parties here weren't unusual.

Despite the suspicion he'd somehow tricked her into this, Harriet took a seat and warmed her hands by the electric fire. The pleasant warmth seeping into her bones reminded her of how it had felt walking into Heatherglen after being so alone on the road from London. It was cosy, homely and she wanted to stay here for as long as possible.

'There you go.' Joanie returned with a tray full of tea things and Charles passed a cup to Harriet before taking one for himself.

'Try some of the shortbread. I made it myself.' She prised open a tartan tin full of sugar-dusted Christmas-tree shapes.

Surmising the sugar hit might help her wooziness, Harriet helped herself. One bite and she was in buttery, sugary heaven.

'You know, I should be sick to death of eating this stuff, but this is really good.' Charles finished his shortbread in two bites.

Joanie blushed, as most women did when Charles paid them a compliment.

'Everyone seemed to like it. Perhaps I should start selling it.'

'You should. It's delicious.' Harriet took another when their host offered the tin around a second time.

Joanie beamed at the praise. 'You two finish your tea. I'm just going to take the rubbish out into the back yard.'

The sudden chill blasting through the building when Joanie opened the door was a stark reminder of the outside temperature.

Charles set down his tea and rubbed Harriet's shoulders up and down as she shivered, trying to generate some heat back into her body. It was the touch of his hands on her that managed to raise her temperature again.

A thud and the sound of broken glass outside startled them both.

'Joanie? Are you all right out there?' Charles called, on his way to find out for himself with Harriet following close behind.

There was no reply and when they were faced with the scene in the shop's back yard they could see why. She was lying unconscious on the ground, the contents of the rubbish bag strewn around her and a pool of blood staining the ground crimson around her head.

Harriet no longer cared about the cold or the snow as she knelt in it to take the woman's pulse. 'Joanie? Can you hear me?'

'I'll phone for an ambulance. Hopefully there'll be one nearby. Watch out for the broken glass. I don't want you getting hurt too.' His concern for her continued to amaze Harriet when it came so naturally to him to think about her. It took her right back to the time when they'd been in love and he'd have done anything to keep her safe.

Harriet carried out basic checks on Joanie, making sure her airways were clear, while Charles gave their location to the switchboard operator. He came to assist her once he hung up, covering Joanie with his coat to keep her warm.

'She's probably slipped on the ice and hit her head in the fall. We don't want to move her until we can get a neck brace on her.' There were all sorts of complications with head or neck injuries and there was a risk of paralysis if they tried to move her.

'We're going to need a CT scan to see what the damage is in case it's more than concussion. If the roads are too bad to get her as far as Glasgow we can make her comfortable at Heatherglen until it's safe to transfer her to hospital.'

'There's a good strong pulse and her breathing is normal.' Harriet reported her observations, but Charles didn't seem as positive as he checked the head wound.

'She has a compound fracture to the skull. The skin and tissue are broken, leaving the brain partially exposed.' An open fracture presented a risk of bacterial infection. If left untreated it could lead to permanent brain damage or even death. An open head injury also left the patient vulnerable to other conditions such as seizures and paralysis.

They needed a CT scan to assess the extent and severity of the fracture, but it was looking as though Joanie was going to require surgery to reduce swelling in the brain. This was time sensitive.

* * *

Harriet was applying pressure around the wound to control the bleeding, all the while talking to the patient and trying unsuccessfully to get a response. Charles got back on the phone to give an update on the severity of their patient's condition, but he didn't return with good news.

'The weather's bad out there. They don't know how long it will take to transfer her to the hospital and an air ambulance is out of the question until that blizzard outside passes.' He had a decision to make quickly as he could already hear the clinic vehicle drawing near. Joanie didn't even have any family around with whom he could discuss the situation.

'We'll take her back to Heatherglen and do a CT scan there.' If it proved he was worrying unnecessarily, they could take their time with the hospital transfer. However, something more serious would require immediate action. They didn't usually carry out major operations at the clinic, referring serious cases to the hospital, but they did act as a local A and E when necessary.

'Lyle will assess her, but we might have to ask for your skills here if we need to operate.' His fellow Scot was the one called on for any local emergencies, but Harriet was the surgeon here. This decision could prevent them wasting time and improve Joanie's chances of recovery. They could make a difference.

This was exactly the sort of situation he'd helped Lyle set the clinic up for in the first place.

CHAPTER SEVEN

THEY WERE GREETED at the front door of the castle by Dr Sinclair and Dr Kirkpatrick.

'I thought you might need some extra help on this one,' Max was offering his services too, which could only improve Joanie's chances with so many accomplished medical staff available.

Harriet realised she'd already been included in this band of doctors. She was no longer merely a visitor.

'Do you mind if I take the lead on this one?' Harriet asked as they wheeled Joanie inside.

'Not at all. You're the surgeon here.' There was no sign of territoriality from Lyle, which went some way to easing the pressure Harriet was suddenly under.

'We'll need a CT scan to see what we're dealing with.'

'Would you like me to assist if you do have to operate?

'The more the merrier, right?' Harriet soon found herself scrubbed in alongside the others prepping for surgery once the scans showed their fears had been justified.

'I'm glad we had so many hands available.' Charles managed to lighten the mood a little as the team came together to provide access to Joanie's injury once she was under general anaesthetic.

He made the initial cranial incision to reveal the extent of the fracture, and he needed assistance to keep the skin flap pinned back out of the way.

Harriet worked quickly to debride the area, cleaning and removing the blood clots that had formed there and repairing damaged blood vessels. Once the bleeding had stopped, she used screws to hold the skull back together in place.

'We'll monitor for infection or secondary complications such as intracranial pressure and brain swelling. Charles, we'll need to keep her on a ventilator until it's possible to move her to a high-dependency unit.' Sometimes patients needed additional surgery to relieve pressure and drain any accumulating blood. In the meantime, she'd prescribe strong antibiotics and medication to reduce possible inflammation.

This wasn't her area of expertise, but she'd spent sufficient time in an operating theatre to be confident in what she was doing. Charles too had put his trust in her skills to make this call. Everything he did was with his patients in mind and whatever would produce the best possible outcome. The easiest option would've been for him to leave Joanie at the mercy of the time it would take to get her to that hospital.

Instead, he'd taken on the responsibility for her initial treatment and everything that would happen once she was at Heatherglen. Harriet was beginning to see there was a role here for her to perform emergency surgery when it was required. Along with the everyday cases which came into the clinic requiring her expertise as an orthopaedic surgeon. It was a good balance of cases which would hold her interest and provide a necessary service to the local community.

All the same, she'd be happier when Joanie was getting specialist care at the hospital and she was relieved of her responsibility.

With the benefit of hindsight, and an explanation for his behaviour, she was beginning to understand what had driven Charles to do the things he'd done in the past. It was a pity it had come so late.

She was the one who'd been selfish over the years, wanting him to herself when he'd devoting himself to improving the lives of countless others.

'I'm sure you weren't expecting to perform brain surgery on your holiday.' Unbidden, Charles brought her a cup of tea and set it on the table beside her chair.

'This was never supposed to be a holiday, remember?' She was keen to remind him that this stay wasn't about her taking some time out. It was for them to make life-changing decisions regarding the child they were to have in a few months' time.

He took the seat opposite, the glow from

the fire throwing shadows on his face. It was the first she'd seen him rest since Joanie's accident. After the surgery he'd insisted she come back home while he oversaw Joanie in Recovery. She'd had the chance to shower, change and take a nap before he'd come back. If this was his regular schedule it was no wonder he didn't have time for a private life, but that didn't mean she was willing to pick up the slack.

'How could I forget when Heatherglen is all about family for me?' He was staring into the flickering flames of the fire, not seeing Harriet at all and making it difficult for her to believe she was part of that sentiment.

'Forgive me, Charles, but I don't understand that. We could've been raising a family together by now, but you turned your back on me and our future. I admire your dedication to your work, but I can't help worrying where you're going to fit a child into your routine? What's going to change?' It was all very well saying the words but what point was there in making promises he couldn't keep? Relegating her in his affections in favour of Heatherglen was one thing but she wouldn't let him do that to their child.

'Nothing. I'm going to remain as faithful to my family as I have been for these last years. That includes my son or daughter.'

A lead weight dropped into Harriet's stomach as he confirmed she'd never been, and never would be, included in that beloved circle.

'Being faithful, providing a home and financial stability is completely different from being a parent. I grew up believing my thoughts and feelings didn't matter in comparison to my mother's. I had to be the strong one and ignore those things every other child took for granted. I didn't have attention, affection or even an interest in what I was doing at school from my mother. So much of my time was taken up with her insecurities and demands for my attention and it was almost a relief when she passed away. I'm not going to subject my own child to the same treatment.'

Losing a parent was anyone's worst nightmare and she still grieved for her mother. It was difficult to reconcile that with the belief that her mother's heart attack had given Harriet her freedom. She would never have reached the heights in her career she had if she was still at her mother's beck and call.

Harriet would do her damnedest to ensure her own child's emotional needs were met. Something she'd missed out on as a child, and as an adult. Sometimes being read a bedtime story or an afternoon spent making cupcakes could be enough to prove to a child it was loved. Since she'd arrived here Charles had gone out of his way to make her comfortable, but it was impossible to know if taking time out when necessary could be sustained long term. There was no way she was going to move here if they'd end up resenting the intrusion into each other's lives, with their child in the middle of the feud.

'I'm aware I'm not part of the family, you made that abundantly clear when you sent me back to London.' It hurt, regardless of his reasons for behaving the way he had after the funeral, or her insistence she was over it.

Charles shook his head. 'Don't you see? I'm the reason my father died. That's why I had to stay at Heatherglen. After we lost

Nick I carried on with my life in London without a thought to how my parents were coping. The long and short of it is that they weren't.

'Dad threw himself into work here, trying to blot out the pain of losing his firstborn. If I'd been any sort of son to him I would've come back and helped then, lightened the load or given him something to focus on other than his grief. He worked himself into an early grave and I did nothing to stop it. I was so used to having my freedom, with none of the responsibilities resting on Nick's shoulders, I simply continued doing my own thing. Including proposing to a vulnerable young woman barely into her twenties who'd only recently lost her mother.'

He was clutching at the arms of the armchair so hard Harriet was afraid he'd rip them off.

'We were both old enough to know what we were doing. Yes, we may have rushed into things but don't use me to exacerbate your guilt. As to your father's death, what could you have done? You were grieving for your brother too.' She remembered the tears and sleepless nights in the wake of Nick's death. Unsurprising in the circumstances. What had happened to his brother had been horrific and traumatic for everyone.

Charles stopped worrying the upholstery and began pacing the room, coming to rest his hands on the mantelpiece and staring into the blazing hearth.

'That wasn't grief. It was guilt.'

Despite the heat of the fire, Harriet shivered at the coldness of his tone. So matter-of-fact and emotionless when she knew Nick's death had devastated him.

'How can you be to blame for his death? He was in Afghanistan on patrol. You didn't plant the IED. I know how much you loved him.' He'd always spoken of Nick with such admiration she was sorry she'd never got to meet the man in person.

'You don't understand…we rowed before he was posted. I said unforgivable things that I can never take back. I told him to drop dead when he tried to lecture me about stepping up and doing my bit to support Heatherglen. All because I was jealous of him. I didn't see why I should put time and effort into the place when I wasn't the golden child who'd be inheriting everything.' The sound that came out of his mouth was somewhere between a laugh and a sob.

'We all say things we don't mean in the heat of the moment. We shouldn't spend the rest of our lives beating ourselves up about it.' She was pretty sure she'd said she'd hated Charles on more than one occasion when emotions had run high, but she'd never stopped loving him. It was a way of lashing out, trying to hurt him with words she knew weren't true.

'We can when we'll never get the chance to take the words back again. I thought he was the one who had everything. He was the war hero, the heir to Heatherglen. Esme was the youngest, Mum and Dad's little princess, and I was nothing more than the spare.' There was such raw pain in his every word it was heartbreaking to listen to and Harriet knew deep in her soul he'd never shared his torment with anyone else. She felt privileged but she also hurt for him, and for herself. If he'd only confided in her at the time they might have worked through this together then.

Instead, they'd retreated to their respective homes and locked themselves away to recover from their wounds.

She wouldn't have been human if she'd sat back and let him pour out his heart without offering some comfort. With his mother no longer on the scene either, and his big-brother protectiveness of Esme, Harriet recognised the signs of self-neglect. Thankfully, she was able to prescribe the correct treatment.

Charles angled his body to meet her when she put a hand on his shoulder to let him know she was there, and pulled him into a hug. He was unyielding at first but soon relaxed into her with a sigh, letting that tension escape on a heavy breath near her ear.

They stood for a while, drawing comfort from each other, with only the sound of the crackling fire to break the silence.

'You have to leave the past behind, Charles. Don't let it destroy you. You're still entitled to a life of your own. Especially when you've done so much for others.' Her voice was cracking with the thought of him carrying so much unnecessary guilt.

'I couldn't bring Nick or Dad back, but I thought I could do the right thing by you, Harriet. Thinking I could get married and have a normal life was a fantasy and the nightmare of taking Heatherglen on was stark reality. I envied your freedom when mine had been taken away from me. I didn't want to ruin your life too by dragging you back here and now I've done that anyway. I know I broke your heart, but I broke my own too.' He broke the seal between their bodies to drop his gaze to her belly where their baby was growing by the day.

'I've never done anything I didn't want to do. Except leave you.' She was trying to smile but the overwhelming sadness at the memory wouldn't let her. She hadn't been truly happy since that day.

'I never wanted you to go, Harriet. I thought I was doing the right thing by you, Nick and my dad, by setting this place up.'

'I know.' She rested her forehead against his, wishing someone had bashed their heads together at the time. 'What about you, Charles? What did you want?'

'The only thing I've ever wanted, Harriet. You.' His hands were at her waist now, sending her pulse into overdrive. When she looked into his eyes, saw the blue fire of his truth there, the game was all over.

Her future was undetermined but, at this moment, she knew exactly what she wanted to do. Yet she hesitated, her mouth hovering against his, her breathing ragged, knowing that if she gave in again to temptation she'd never want to leave.

Then Charles closed the gap and made the decision for her, his lips hard on hers as he kissed her. She'd been waiting for this since London. Wanting him to kiss her and obliterate everything else around them. Now she was burning with need for more. Circumstances had kept them apart for too long and now that raw passion for each other was free to burn out of control.

Harriet tugged his shirt from the waistband of his trousers, undoing only a few buttons before yanking it over his head. Much to Charles's amusement.

'Here? Now?'

'Yes.' She didn't recognise the huskiness in her voice demanding Charles take her where she stood. Such was the intensity of her desire to have this man again she'd lost all inhibitions.

She let her hands roam over his torso, getting to know that terrain of hair and muscle. Charles kissed his way along her neck as he tore off her clothes. 'Max and Esme are in bed and Dougal is safely locked up,' he murmured against her fevered skin. So they weren't being totally reckless. This time.

The yearning to join together was as great as it had been in London. Yet that urgency to consummate their reunion before common sense prevailed had been replaced with a different longing. This transcended the physical, it was more than re-creating the best times they'd had together. Now they were going to be parents, making plans for some sort of future together, they were reconnecting on an emotional level too.

Harriet could try and deny it. Blame it on her hormones or a holiday fling, but Charles was the only man she'd ever given herself to completely. Her body and soul had always been his and in sleeping with him again she was playing a dangerous game with her heart.

To her detriment she'd always considered Charles worth the risk.

Hopefully, this time it would pay off. With the baby, the job and an offer to stay at Heatherglen, the last commitment he needed to make to her was himself. It was the only reason she'd stay. She loved him. Always had and always would. Without having that in return from him there was no way she could live here. It would be so much worse than never seeing him again.

'Are you cold?' He mistook her shiver as a symptom of being left clad only in her underwear when she was burning for him from the inside out.

'Nervous,' she answered honestly. Anxious about what was going to happen between them after tonight. She needed to be more than a convenient distraction for him.

'Me too.' His admission surprised her. It suggested there was more on the line for him too than simple physical satisfaction.

Charles took her back into his embrace, brushed the hair back from her face. 'We can take it slowly.'

As if to prove they had all the time in the world, he gave her a long, leisurely, skin-tingling kiss that melted any nerves into a puddle.

He unclipped her bra and let it fall to the floor, freeing her breasts to his attentions. Her nipples were more sensitive than usual, and a shot of electricity zapped to every erogenous zone when he brushed his thumb across one. When he took the other in his mouth and tugged, she almost combusted with desire.

'Charles…' She was pushing away his boxers, ridding her of the final barrier to his body. So much for taking it slowly. Her body had decided she wanted him to satisfy her craving right now.

How could something they'd done a hundred times in the past still feel like the first time? Charles wanted this to last and to make it special. The night they'd conceived this baby had been passionate and urgent because they'd thought they'd never see each other again. Tonight he was going to make love to the mother of his baby, proving his commitment to her. No pressure.

He could already see the subtle changes in her body with the swell and new sensitivity of her breasts. It awakened such a love inside him for her it terrified him that he might hurt her all over again. He wanted to put her needs before his own so he could watch the pleasure on her face and know he'd put it there.

Not that Harriet was making it easy for him. Her confident command of his body as she slid her hands over his backside and around to take hold of him was seriously jeopardising his good intentions.

'Don't worry. I'm going to make sure you get everything you need, Harriet.' He quelled his own throbbing desire to focus on hers.

He dotted feather-light kisses across her midriff, felt her quiver against his lips as he moved lower until he was kneeling between her feet. With a gentle nudge he parted her legs and relocated his focus to her inner thighs, kissing and teasing the soft skin. Her sweet gasp of anticipation and the slight unsteadiness in her stance matched his own growing impatience for that most intimate contact.

She opened to him at the touch of his tongue and cried out as he lapped her sex. Hands braced on his shoulders, she encouraged his efforts and he lost himself in the quest for her orgasm with every venture into her core.

He was so dedicated to his pursuit that when Harriet climaxed he almost came apart with her. Through every tightening and subsequent release of her inner muscles he demanded everything she had, leaving her limp and breathless when the last shudder of her climax subsided.

He didn't give her the time to say anything, literally sweeping her off her feet to carry her over to the settee. Softly, he laid her down and covered her naked body with his. Kissed her until he drove himself to the brink of insanity with desire for her.

'Harriet, I can't wait any longer.'

'Good.' The coy smile was at odds with

the wanton action of her legs as she snaked them around his hips. Pressed tightly against him, it was impossible for Charles to resist any more. Finally, he gave in to his own primal urge and took possession of the woman he loved. If he'd thought she'd believe him, he would've said the words. Instead, he wanted to show her the strength of those feelings in his every move.

He claimed her again and again, her soft moans increasing his steady rhythm until his restraint was hanging by a thread. Then Harriet secured her inner hold around him, building that unrelenting pressure inside him to the point where he could no longer hold back.

He roared as his love for her burst free, so loudly he was afraid they might hear him at the other side of the castle. Perspiration clung to his skin as the ripples of his release shuddered through his limbs.

Only then did he see the sheen of tears in Harriet's eyes and his racing heart almost came to a halt.

'What's wrong? Did I hurt you?' He'd been

carried away on that wave of ecstasy, but he was sure she'd been right there with him.

She bit her lip and shook her head, letting him breathe again. He'd never have forgiven himself if he'd done something to cause her pain for a second time in her life.

'It was amazing. It's just…' Her throat sounded raw with the unshed tears she was swallowing down for his sake. He understood then why she was so upset. They could have had this a long time ago and no one knew better than he what a great loss that had been.

'I know.' He kissed her on the lips, trying to show her how sorry he was as the salt water of her tears washed over them both.

All this time they could've been living at Heatherglen together, raising their family. The hurt he'd caused them both seemed senseless now in the scheme of things. The separation clearly hadn't diminished their feelings for each other. They were more intense than ever.

Dougal barked somewhere outside the confines of their reunion, reminding Charles that their privacy wasn't guaranteed. More so when he heard a bedroom door opening and closing, followed by footsteps on the stairs.

Without another word they scrabbled for their clothes like two horny teenagers about to be sprung by his parents. They dressed in silence, but remained undisturbed by his sister or her puppy charge. As he pulled on his trousers, and Harriet fastened the last button on her blouse, no one would've been able to tell they'd just had the most mind-blowing sex. Or that he'd woken up to the fact he loved her more now than he ever had as that selfish young student. Perhaps the time apart hadn't been a complete tragedy. If not for the life he'd gone on to have without her he might not have appreciated how much more enriched it was with her in it.

'We can go to my room. We'll have more privacy there.' Not only so he could share his bed with her but they had to talk about the future. Time was slipping away and he wanted to spend every second of it with her. To make her feel the same way about him so she'd realise this was the best place for her and the baby. With him.

'If you don't mind, I think I'll retire to my own room, Charles. I don't want to confuse anyone.' The willing partner he'd had wrapped around his body only moments ago was now keeping her distance, her hands fidgeting in her lap.

His earlier euphoria dissipated with the rejection, though he didn't think this was about revenge. It was much something much more serious than that. Doubt.

'I just thought—'

'Please don't put me under any more pressure. It's not fair.' She was on the verge of crying again and he would never willingly cause her distress again.

'I'll see you in the morning, then.' It was almost as difficult to walk away from her tonight as it had been all those years ago. Only this time he was leaving the next move to her. The decision about the future of their relationship was entirely down to Harriet. He was powerless. Something he was no longer used to.

CHAPTER EIGHT

'ESME IS LOOKING forward to meeting you to discuss the possibility of a therapy dog for Bryony.' Harriet had caught up with Bryony's parents in the corridor and taken them aside to discuss their daughter's needs. She didn't want to mention anything in front of her and get her hopes up in case things didn't work out.

'Yes, Charles said he'd make an appointment for us to see her at the therapy centre. We think it's a great idea. A dog will be good company for Bryony.' Her mother was much brighter than she'd been yesterday, and Harriet imagined the prospect of training a dog had caused much excitement.

'I'm so pleased to hear that before I go back to London.'

'I suppose you have your own family there.'

A denial hovered on Harriet's lips, but they weren't here to discuss her personal life. It was already confusing things at the clinic. Instead, she simply smiled, neither confirming nor denying the assumption she had someone to return to. She wasn't sure if it was sadder to admit that or the fact she was running away from the chance to have a family here because the idea freaked her out so much.

Bryony's parents thanked her for her help before setting off back home, leaving Harriet wondering where she could retreat for peace of mind from Charles.

She'd set out early this morning to avoid him. It was silly, really, when she was living in his castle and seeing patients. She couldn't dodge him, or what was happening between them, for ever. It had crossed her mind to do a moonlit flit and leave in the middle of the night. All because sleeping with him again had made her realise she was still in love with him. In reality there was no escaping that, regardless of her location.

She dropped her head into her hands, taking a moment to reflect on what the hell she was doing with Charles. Once she'd had that space from him to think straight last night she'd convinced herself that by refocusing on the professional aspect of her stay she could get away unscathed. It wasn't turning out to be that simple, though. There was no way to keep this solely about the baby now they'd slept together again.

It was one thing to tell herself she'd somehow exaggerated how great their last time together had been and she'd read more into it than she should have for a conference hookup. The reality of being in his home and work life was very different. Those feelings weren't simply going to be cured by hiding from him.

She'd spent half the morning with Esme, playing with the dogs and discussing the merits of pairing therapy pets with CP patients, safe in the knowledge Charles was on his rounds at the clinic. She'd only come back here when she'd spotted him going back home. It would be childish, not to mention exhausting, to keep this up. He'd catch up with her at some point.

Then what? She couldn't tell him why she'd run off after their passionate encounter and expect things to carry on as normal. Either he'd try to take advantage of her wasted feelings towards him in order to maintain contact with his child or he could cut off communication altogether. One thing was for sure, he didn't return the strength of her admiration, he never had.

Harriet was stuck, trapped by her own emotions and bad decisions. The worst of it was she didn't regret last night, and she'd do it again given the chance. She was a danger to herself.

The quiet elegance of the lounge called to her. A room where patients were able to relax and interact and which had been empty when she'd passed by earlier.

'Sorry. I didn't realise anyone was in here.' She hadn't expected to see another peace-seeker but there was a man sitting by the fire.

'No problem. It's a good place to collect your thoughts.' Now he'd spoken to her it would be rude to walk out again so Harriet joined him on the opposite side of the fireplace.

'I'm not sure I should be collecting them. I might be better off throwing them in the bin.' That prompted a deep laugh and she instantly relaxed in the man's company.

'Are you staying here?'

'I'm visiting with Charles and Esme.'

'Oh, you're a friend of the family? You knew Nick, then?'

'Unfortunately, I never got to meet him. Was he a friend of yours?'

There was a sad nod of the head, which went a long way to explaining the extent to which his death had affected the man. 'I served with him in Afghanistan. Not an easy thing to get over.'

'I'm so sorry.'

'At least I can talk about it without breaking down now.' His self-deprecating humour was much appreciated by Harriet when she knew nothing she could say would ease the suffering he'd gone through.

'They've been helping you here, then?' If he was a friend of Nick's she knew Charles and Esme would have bent over backwards to assist this man with whatever ailed him.

'They've been life-savers. They literally got me back on my feet and now we're working on getting me integrated back into society. I've still got an issue with loud noises I'm dealing with. You know, with the whole bombs and explosions thing that I can't seem to get out of my head.'

'That must be awful but I'm sure you're making great progress. These things just take time.' It was great to hear first hand the difference they were making here, and she was sure Charles would puff up with pride when she recounted the conversation to him.

'I'm very grateful for the help Charles and Esme, and all of the staff here have given me. We're working up to the ultimate test soon. They're planning a firework display for Hogmanay, so we'll see how I go with that.' He lifted a pair of crutches from the floor and heaved himself into a standing position. Harriet hoped she hadn't chased him away with her arrival.

'Good luck.'

'Thanks. I'm Andy, by the way. Andy Wallace.'

'Harriet Bell.' She couldn't remember the last time she'd shaken so many hands and made so many new friends in such a short time. It was a nice feeling, being part of the community.

'I hope I see you around again soon, Harriet.'

If the lounge was intended to give the residents here a time out from their stresses and allow them a space to simply relax, it had definitely achieved its goal today. It had helped to take her mind off her own problems to think about someone else's.

'I've just spoken to Bryony's parents. They're very excited.' Charles's voice disturbed Harriet's chance of peace and quiet.

'So it seems. I'm glad they'll have something to look forward to.'

'I wanted to speak to you about that.' He sat down beside her on the love seat, which was suddenly crowded now he'd wedged his large frame so completely into the space. There was no room for her to edge away from him when they were sitting hip to hip and thigh to thigh. It was ridiculous that in a castle of this size she couldn't put some distance between them. After all these years apart, suddenly they were drawn together at every turn.

'About Bryony?'

'Partly. I take it you've heard of selective dorsal rhizotomy?' They weren't the words she'd expected to hear from Charles today, but they managed to spark her interest all the same.

'Yes. It's a spinal procedure used to improve mobility. I've been involved in a few.' It involved cutting nerves close to the spinal column, which could not only reduce spasticity but give patients back their independence. However, it came with risks. The operation was irreversible and relied on only cutting sensory nerves. If motor nerves were severed it could result in total paralysis. It was a highly specialised surgery, but she had seen some life-changing improvements for patients who'd had it.

'So you know the difference it could make to someone like Bryony? A lot of CP patients could benefit from it so they're not relying on hoists for the rest of their lives, or they're able to do simple tasks for themselves such as feeding and drinking.'

'Charles, I couldn't make that decision. There's a lengthy screening process for those being considered for the procedure. Patients have to be assessed by physical and occupational therapists on their functionality. My involvement is mostly on a post-op basis should any problems arise with joint alignment. Ultimately the final say would be down to the neurosurgeon performing the procedure and there's no guarantee it would work in her case anyway.' Everyone was assessed on an individual basis and as much as she wanted to improve life for the little girl and alleviate her pain, it wasn't up to her.

'I know I'd have to consult a neurosurgeon too. If I hadn't had Heatherglen to run I might have gone into surgery myself. There's a lot of things I would have done differently given the chance but this is about looking forward, not back. I'd like to give families like Bryony's hope.'

'One of the problems is that there's very little funding out there for the procedure.

We're in a Catch-22 situation where they won't approve it universally until they can see conclusive results that it works. Hospitals only have approval for a limited number who meet certain criteria.'

'That's why I want to look into part-funding it myself. Perhaps set up a research facility here, with your help, where we can provide the procedure to those who need it and catalogue the results.'

'Patients need intensive physiotherapy after surgery to help with their mobility too.' This wasn't something to be taken on without considering all the implications and the potential benefits had to be deemed greater than the risks.

'Of course. I'd have to look into extending the physiotherapy department too. I'll sound Flora out about that. What do you think? Would you be interested in being part of it?'

'It's an amazing opportunity, but there would have to be something more concrete in place before I could consider giving up everything in London. You would have to have a neurosurgeon on board or this whole thing is moot.' They could do so much good for patients across the board and it sounded like an exciting project. Every physician wanted to be part of something revolutionary in the medical world and Harriet was no exception. She simply had to be sure there was something career-wise worth moving for if things didn't work out for her here on a personal level.

'I know a few in the field who are interested in taking part if we have the appropriate after care in place, which would include an orthopaedic surgeon. In the meantime, I'll get a proposal together and get things moving. I'll make some enquiries with Bryony's consultant too and see if she could be a possible candidate.'

'It would be great for her and her family. They've been on my mind a lot.'

'I thought I hadn't seen much of you since last night.' He rested his hand on her knee and though it was an innocent touch compared to last night, her body didn't appear to understand that. Her skittish pulse was reacting as though they were still rolling around naked on the couch. It didn't help when he was expecting her to say something about the progression of their relationship now it was more than resolving custody of their unborn child.

'I've been busy sussing out the career potential here.' It wasn't a total lie. She'd simply been using that research to keep her out of harm's way. When Charles was close she didn't give any thought to the consequences of her actions. Knew only that she wanted him.

She'd never had much time for relationships, but it was different with Charles. Yes, she had needs, and goodness knew he increased hers every time she laid eyes on him but being intimate with him was about so much more than meeting her physical needs.

Perhaps it was their history, and now their future as parents, but she hadn't realised how incomplete she'd felt until she'd come back to Heatherglen and found that missing part of her. A return to London now would only emphasise what she was lacking in her life. If only she could be truly sure she could trust Charles again she would rather stay here in some sort of relationship with him than go back to a world without him in it at all.

'And? What's the verdict?' He lifted his hand as he awaited her response and even that loss was too great for her to bear for too long.

Harriet cleared her throat, but her mind wasn't proving as easy. She had to work hard to focus on her career prospects rather than on the man beside her. 'I can see the possibilities Heatherglen has to offer.'

'Such as?' His mouth twitched, and it was apparent he knew exactly where her lustful imagination was taking her.

She crossed her legs and attempted to stem the arousal threatening to wreak havoc inside her. 'The clinic provides a good base for my work. As you said, I can consult and operate at the hospital when I'm needed. Working with Esme at the therapy centre is appealing too. I think it would be mutually beneficial for us to confer about patients. Bryony's opened my eyes to the possibility of putting patients in touch with Esme and vice versa. We could do so much together.'

This was what he'd planned when he'd

pushed her towards his patients, but she would've seen the benefits for herself eventually. Heatherglen was offering her the chance to continue her career at the same time as raising a family. The only thing casting a shadow over proceedings was that fear of having her heart ripped out again.

'And us?' He took one of her fidgeting hands in his, stroking the inside of her wrist with his thumb and sending shivers of delight across her skin.

A lifetime of denying herself the pleasures he could give her or trying to keep a lid on her feelings was a choice she didn't want to make but Charles hadn't voiced any desire to have a proper relationship. They were going to be parents. They'd already been lovers. It was as much commitment as he was liable to make and only Harriet could decide if that would be enough for her.

'I see no reason why we shouldn't carry on as we are.' The thought of sharing his bed regularly emboldened her gaze on him. Knowing if she wavered he'd see through the bravado and realise she wanted more than he was prepared to give.

'So you'll stay? We'll raise the baby here, together?' The hope and joy she saw on his face should've made her decision clear cut, but it caused a wobble in her confidence. He wasn't declaring his love for her, he was excited about having the baby here.

'I'll stay for now, but I still have to go back to London in the new year as planned.' Despite her unrequited feelings for Charles she knew this was probably a better environment in which to nurture a child than the lonely existence she had in London. As future parents that's what they both wanted.

'What about a permanent move?'

'I'm seriously thinking about it...'

'You don't know how happy that makes me.' To demonstrate, he cupped her face in his hands and planted a kiss on her lips.

If Harriet closed her eyes she could make herself believe this was possible.

When Charles was kissing her, when his hands were on her, she was able to live in the moment. She could move here, raise their child, keep her career, and make love with Charles when the mood took her. The only thing she couldn't have was his love, but no one had it all. Perhaps she simply had to settle for what she could get.

'Morning, sleepyhead.' Charles nuzzled into Harriet's hair, tousled from sleep and their other nocturnal activities.

'Is it that time already?' she murmured, half-asleep.

This was everything he'd dreamed about. Waking up to a naked Harriet at the start of the day, falling back into bed with her at night was the perfect way to begin and end his days. He had the clinic and now, with Harriet here and a baby on the way, he considered himself the luckiest man on the planet.

''Fraid so.'

'Ugh.' She snuggled further down under the covers and Charles's heart swelled because she'd rather be here with him than anywhere else. Long may it last.

These past couple of days with Harriet had been amazing. It wasn't the traditional start to a relationship, beginning with a pregnancy and working backwards. In time he hoped they could repair their personal issues so she could trust him again and someday they'd be living here as a proper family. Not merely together through circumstances. So far Harriet hadn't given him any indication she wanted anything other than having her physical needs met. Although he was happy to oblige, he was still in love with her, he always had been. He hoped at some point in the near future she'd feel the same way about him.

'We do have a bit of time before I have to do my rounds.' Every part of him was wide awake now.

She blinked her eyes open as he nibbled her ear lobes and brushed his thumb across her nipple. He knew all her weak spots and wasn't afraid to use that knowledge to his advantage.

'I look a mess.'

'You look beautiful.' She looked so at peace he wouldn't want her any other way.

'I…have…morning…breath.' She giggled in between kisses.

'I…don't…care.' He didn't. Not that she tasted anything but sweet on Charles's tongue. All that mattered was that she was here with him.

'In that case—'

It was his turn to gasp as Harriet stroked the length of his manhood, making him aware she was up for whatever he had in mind.

His playful growl was answered by her squeal of surprise as he flipped her onto her back. Once he was covering her body with his, all joking was finished. Making love to Harriet was a serious business.

She was so ready for him Charles slipped easily inside her to find that peace he'd only ever found with Harriet. She'd been the only woman he'd ever considered sharing his life with. Although that thought process in the past had been behind the decision to break up, the idea now was akin to winning the lottery. Every touch, every kiss from her was a gift. Someday he hoped they'd both believe he was worthy.

He wanted to say the words, to tell her he loved her, but he didn't have the right. It would scare her off when she'd been wary enough of this set-up. After that first night together, she'd done her best to avoid him until she'd seemed to come to the conclusion this arrangement would be convenient. His feelings for her were anything but convenient. They'd complicated the life he had at Heatherglen and the one he'd planned with the mother of his child. If he kept them to himself, they couldn't hurt anyone. It was only thinking of himself that caused pain to those around him.

'Hey.' Harriet's voice broke through his thoughts. She took his head in her hands and forced him to look at her. 'Where did you go?'

He had to get better at pretending he could be casual about this if he expected her to stick around.

'I'm right here with you.' He kissed her long and deep, sufficiently that the tension ebbed away from her limbs again beneath him. Passion enough to distract them both from what was going on in his head.

They rocked together, clinging onto what they had in the moment. As Charles followed Harriet over the edge, his last thought before oblivion hit was that since she had come back, his heart had begun to heal again.

In the end they'd had to rush to get ready in time for work, they'd spent so long in bed.

'I'm going to have to get changed. I can't turn up in yesterday's clothes.'

He'd tried to pull her back in for one last smooch, but she wasn't having any of it.

'You could borrow something of mine. I don't think anyone would object if you turned up wearing one of my shirts and nothing else.' He drew a finger down her spine as she leaned over the side of the bed to collect her discarded clothes.

'I would,' she protested, but he couldn't help going back for more when he'd made her shiver. He swept her hair from the back of her neck and danced kisses along that ticklish spot. Her response as she leaned back for more of his touch only added fuel to the fire in his belly. Charles reached around to cup her breasts in his palms, pinching her nipples between thumbs and forefingers so she groaned with appreciation.

'I really have to go,' she tried again as he nuzzled her neck.

'You don't have to. You're free to do as you want, and I hope to hell that includes me.' He knew he'd said the wrong thing when she stiffened beneath him and covered his hands with hers to stop them wandering any further.

'Charles, if I become part of this household I'm not going to take advantage of my position, and neither are you. I'll be coming here to work, not be installed as your mistress.' Harriet pulled her clothes on with such jerky movements Charles could see she was battling to contain her temper.

'I know that. It was a joke. A bad one.'

She wasn't listening as she walked barefoot to the door with her shoes in her hands, no longer content to spend another second with him to put them on.

'I'll see you at the clinic.' The slamming door said everything about the offence he'd caused.

Charles fell back onto the pillows with a sigh. It shouldn't be a crime to want to spend time with her, but it wasn't something she apparently wanted to hear. Perhaps he'd oversold Heatherglen to her when it now held more appeal for her than him.

CHAPTER NINE

HARRIET KNEW SHE'D overreacted to Charles's teasing this morning. Especially when she'd have happily spent the rest of the day in bed with him. It was that niggling fear in the pit of her stomach that sex was all she was good for that made her snap.

'I'm going to have to tell him how I feel.' She ruffled Dougal's ears as he lay at her feet. With Charles caught up in admin work, something she couldn't help him with, she'd returned to his private quarters. It didn't stop him plaguing her thoughts.

Since coming here Charles had dominated her every waking moment, and a lot of the sleeping ones. It was no wonder when he was the reason she'd come here. He was always going to be her baby's father. For her own peace of mind she was going to have to face the consequences of these feelings, even if it meant the end of the affair.

'At least I'm not the only who's fallen for him.' As a last resort to stop Dougal running riot in the clinic in his pursuit of Charles, Esme had suggested using one of his old shirts as a comforter for the pup. It had done the trick. The scent of his reluctant master, lining his basket, settled him until the man himself was available. If things didn't work out Harriet might have to steal some of Charles's clothes to take back to London and do the same.

'It's a poor substitute for the real thing, isn't it?' Although, like the smitten pup, she was sure she'd tire quickly of the imitation.

Dougal snuffled deeper into the shirt, inhaling the scent she knew was intoxicating. They both just wanted to be with him. Unfortunately, it seemed he was only prepared to tolerate either of them on his terms. Yet Harriet had seen him soften towards the dog, sacrificing one of his shirts and fussing over Dougal when he thought she wasn't looking. He was getting used to sharing his space and she hoped that would extend to her. After everything he'd been through with his family, the personal struggles he'd shared with her, it was possible he was simply as scared as she was about getting hurt and losing someone else close.

Dougal let out a pitiful whine.

'It's time to be brave. We've got to show Charles what he could have here. A real family.' She took the dog lead from the hook behind the door and clipped it to Dougal's collar.

'Let's go for a walk.'

Either he'd already learned what the 'W' word meant or he'd picked up on Harriet's renewed optimism, but Dougal was panting with anticipation and jumping at her to hurry up and open the door.

She was going to have a word with Esme about taking Dougal on permanently on Charles's behalf. He'd be the family pet their child could grow up with and a commitment to her future at Heatherglen, where she was more than a staff member or a lover. She wanted to be here as a valued part of Charles's beloved home.

* * *

Charles couldn't wait to get back to Harriet after work. Things between them had been strained since his faux pas that morning and he intended to make amends. It had taken a lot to persuade her this was the place for her and their baby and it wouldn't take much for her to change her mind again. Joking that she was moving here to be a lady of leisure, or pleasure, wasn't going to do much to keep her onside.

As he stood at the window he could see Harriet walking Dougal outside with Max and Esme. His sister and her new beau were effortlessly comfortable together, hand in hand. Whereas he and Harriet veered back and forth in their affections.

Although history didn't paint him in the best light, they shouldn't have to struggle to want to be together in the early days of a relationship. It wasn't something that should have to be forced. Yes, they were compatible in bed, they always had been, but outside that confined space there was more than a physical distance between them.

There was always an excuse or a disagreement between them, sending her running after they'd made love. She was holding back from him and that wasn't a good place from which to start a relationship.

'Hey.' He greeted Harriet with a kiss on the cheek. It was all he could do not to pull her in for a full make-out session after spending all day thinking about her.

The slight uneasiness he could detect in the way she was twisting Dougal's lead around her fingers and the sidelong look she gave his sister stopped him. Clearly, she hadn't been pining for him in the same way as the pup pawing at his trouser leg desperate for his attention.

'Hello. I thought I'd take him out for some fresh air this afternoon.' Harriet wasn't as hesitant about showing affection to the other male in her life as she showered the pup with kisses and petting. 'I didn't have anything else to do.'

He caught hold of her arm before she could follow Esme and Max inside. 'We could go out somewhere for dinner, if you like.'

The thing he didn't want was for her to get bored after only a couple of days here. Although he'd forgotten it over the years, there was a world outside Heatherglen.

Harriet moved on past him. 'Some other time perhaps. I have some things I have to sort out with your sister.'

She didn't elaborate or even acknowledge his desire to take her out. He was getting the brush-off.

'Is there something wrong?' He'd rather know now than go on pretending until after the baby was born.

'Wrong? No. I have to take Dougal in and feed him. Excuse me.' She ducked her head under his arm and scooted inside, trailing Dougal, who was fighting to stay by Charles's side. At least someone wanted to be with him.

Charles had that same horrible emptiness inside that he'd had that day he'd realised he was jeopardising Harriet's future happiness by making her follow him to Heatherglen. It was happening all over again. Today should have been proof that neither he nor Heatherglen were good for her.

Her time in London was precious, a whirlwind of activity. By dangling promises of a better life for their child he'd emotionally blackmailed her into agreeing. Only to have her spend her days walking stray dogs and slipping between his sheets when he wasn't at work. He'd virtually bribed her with that promise of a research facility. It was something he'd been considering since Bryony had come to the clinic but the prospect of having Harriet as part of the team made it even more of a priority.That kind of opportunity would grab someone as ambitious as Harriet, but how long would it take to complete? What could he offer her in the meantime?

He banged his head against the doorframe. He'd been the worst kind of fool, a selfish one. This time running the clinic and the estate had made him forget the implications of dragging someone into it along with him. These years in isolation were worth nothing if he hadn't learned his lesson and he stole Harriet's life anyway for his own benefit.

It wasn't for him to tell her she'd be better off here when he knew nothing of her existence beyond these walls. Only what he'd imagined, and that was never going to be something he considered more fulfilling than this when it meant he'd lose her.

This trial run was supposed to have been a test for her to work out what she wanted. No matter how he tried to convince her otherwise, it didn't include him or Heatherglen. Not long term. He was fine for a holiday fling, but her trust in him hadn't recovered and it never would as long as he continued to ignore what was best for her.

It suited him having her, the woman he loved, on site, looking forward to raising their child together at his family home. Exactly the sort of selfish behaviour that had driven his father and brother to their deaths. He couldn't bear responsibility for destroying the lives of any more of his loved ones.

Okay, Harriet wasn't in immediate danger but being somewhere she didn't want to be, with someone she didn't love, would be like a slow, painful death. Like the one she'd told him her mother had suffered. An existence she'd sworn she'd never submit to. He was making her follow in those footsteps and sacrifice her identity for his sake.

Charles had made that difficult decision

to end things after his father's death because it had been the right thing to do for Harriet. Now it wasn't her feelings about him clouding her judgement, it was those she had for the baby. At his prompting. He didn't believe she was capable of loving him again and it was his fault she was pregnant. If he'd used contraception or common sense, she would never have tracked him down again.

As much as he hated to say it, the Charles who'd set her free the first time had been a better man than the one he'd been recently.

Harriet would've loved to have gone out on a proper date with Charles. She couldn't remember the last time she'd made time for dinner, or even a movie, with someone. Since reconnecting with him they'd spent their quality time together in bed and though she wasn't complaining, it would be nice to venture out as a couple. That getting to know each other stage was needed more than ever when they were such different people from before.

She was sure they'd get another chance for a bit of fun away from Heatherglen now she was making plans for a permanent move. Taking on the responsibility of a family pet would show Charles she wanted to be here long term with their family.

'I'm so happy for you both.' Esme's eyes were shimmering with happy tears as she hugged Harriet, then scooped Dougal up for a cuddle.

'I'm not sure your brother will feel the same but he's more fond of this one than he'll admit.' Harriet had come to Esme's quarters to discuss the adoption. Her living space at the far side of the castle was perfect for having secret puppy conversations.

She wanted to surprise Charles with the news later. It had been on her mind about Dougal for a couple of days but seeing Esme at work, training and teaching Dougal, and her, a few basic commands had convinced her they could tame this little one. After all, he'd become part of the family too.

'Being honest about his feelings isn't a strong point for Charlie boy, but I can see the difference it has made to him, having you here. I'm not about to interfere in whatever is going on between you two but it's obvious you're in love.'

'It is?'

'It's great having my big sis back again.'

Harriet had been so distracted by her relationship with Charles she'd neglected the one she should've been cultivating with Esme. She'd never supposed the few meet-ups they'd had during uni years would've had any lasting impact on Charles's teenage sister but clearly Esme had seen it differently.

'I'm sorry I didn't keep in touch.' Harriet rested her hand on Esme's, wishing she'd attempted to maintain some sort of communication over the years. She'd simply assumed she was no longer welcome at Heatherglen in any shape or form.

Esme shrugged. 'You weren't to know I'd put you on a pedestal and turned you into the big sister I'd always wanted. I was devastated when Charles said you'd gone, and the wedding was off. I had no idea what had happened. Only that I'd lost you on top of Nick and Dad. I was angry at you, and Charles, for quite some time.'

'I'm sorry. I was so devastated by the

break-up I wasn't thinking about anyone's feelings except my own.' Poor Esme had been forgotten about in the midst of the family tragedy and drama. It explained some of the behaviour Harriet had heard about during Esme's teenage years.

'I think we were all floundering back then. Hopefully we've found what we've been looking for.' She glanced at the ring on her pinkie finger.

'You and Max certainly seem very happy.' She and Charles had some way to go yet but there was time before the baby came to work out those issues that got in the way every time they got close.

'It's a promise ring. We want to take our time.' Her excitement was evident, even in Esme's hushed tones. It sounded as though she was afraid to say it out loud and jinx things. Harriet could empathise. She didn't take anything for granted when it came to affairs of the heart.

'Good idea. Congratulations.' This time Harriet instigated the hug.

With Esme confiding in her it felt as though they'd formed their own secret club.

A sisterhood. Suddenly thoughts of girlie gossip and shopping trips filled her head. Neither were things she did on a regular basis, but she'd always thought she'd been missing out. It was the promise of spending time with Esme and extending that notion of family that held so much appeal.

'We've all got so much to look forward to and Heatherglen is beginning to feel like a real home again. Can you imagine what it's going to be like when the baby gets here?'

Harriet didn't have the heart to express her concerns regarding Charles's commitment to her personally. She hoped that was something they could work out and signing up as Dougal's new guardians would show Charles she was thinking of them as a family already.

That fizz of excitement Harriet had been trying to keep under control was bubbling to the surface now she had someone else's enthusiasm to expand on.

'I can't wait until next Christmas and being part of everything here. First I need to talk to Charles and let him know about the plans I'm making.' By this time next year, she'd expect to be fully settled. She and Charles would have taken some time off work to spend time with the baby for its first Christmas.

It was impossible not to get carried away by the idea of family in Esme's company, when she thrived on it. Each of them had suffered in their own way over the years but finally the planets were coming into alignment.

'Harriet?' Charles knocked on the bedroom door and waited for a response. He'd already checked the kitchen and lounge, but there was no answer from Harriet's room either. There'd been no sign of Dougal either since their return. He thought that by the time he'd showered and changed she'd have finished whatever she'd wanted to talk to Esme about without him present. A matter that wounded him more than it should.

She could talk to anyone about whatever she pleased, but it highlighted the growing distance between them if she couldn't confide in him.

He would do his best to reassure her she'd

have whatever support she needed when the baby came, if that was all that was keeping her here.

'Are you there?' He inched the door open in case she was simply avoiding him, but the room was empty.

He took a seat on the end of her bed, expecting her to come back at some point. He didn't want to invade her privacy, but the partially unpacked bag was sitting nearby. She was living out of her luggage and ready to run at a moment's notice. He was hoping his news would give her a better sense of security here.

The pitter-patter of puppy paws sounded down the corridor and the anticipation of facing Harriet made his stomach flip.

'We're going to have to face the music at some point, Dougal. Let's hope Charles is in a better mood than usual.'

He got to his feet, suddenly feeling like the intruder he was as he unintentionally eavesdropped on her talking to the dog. Harriet hadn't always seen him at his best, but he was doing his best to win her over.

'Charles? What are you doing here?' She

pulled up in the doorway, so startled by his appearance that she dropped the dog lead from her grasp.

Cue Dougal and his over-affectionate fascination with Charles's trouser leg. This was one time they didn't require his canine antics providing some light relief.

'Can we do something about this dog so we get five minutes' peace to talk properly?' If this moment proved to be a turning point in their relationship, he didn't want it tainted by the memory of her being more interested in the dog than him.

'Okay. Sure.' She stared at him intently for a few seconds before retrieving Dougal and calling on a passing Esme to come and take care of him for her.

'I know I upset you with that stupid comment about being the lady of the house this morning so I put in a few calls to Fort William Hospital. I have a few contacts and I made enquiries on your behalf about transferring there.'

'You did what?' She crossed her arms, challenging him to spit out the words he was now wondering whether he should say at all.

'I wanted you to have a concrete reason for moving here. I thought securing a position for you at the hospital was the best way to convince you there was a life waiting for you here since the research facilities will take a while to get up and running at the clinic.'

'You didn't think to consult me on this first?' Harriet frowning at him was not the reaction he'd expected.

'I thought you'd be pleased. This is giving you the career opportunities you wanted as part of the conditions of moving here.' Unfortunately, neither he nor Heatherglen had been enough to convince her to stay, which was why he'd used his initiative to go further afield. Over time he hoped she'd develop a love for him on the same par as the one she obviously had for her job. Except the impatient tapping of her foot on the floor said she wasn't best pleased with this turn of events.

'Charles, something as huge as changing my career path is for me to decide, not you.' She huffed out an exasperated breath. 'This is you making decisions for me again, without considering the consequences. I know nothing about this hospital, what their practices are like, or what I'd be expected to do in that particular environment. Things that are down to me to investigate, if and when I'm ready to relocate.'

Charles was beginning to think he couldn't do right for doing wrong.

'I was simply trying to facilitate that move for you. All I want is for you to have a reason to want to stay here.'

'Is it me or the baby you want here?'

'I thought you came as a package?' He tried, and failed, to make her smile because he wasn't sure which answer she wanted to hear. Of course it was important for him to be close to the baby but more than anything it was his desire to have Harriet here with him that had prompted his flurry of phone calls today.

'This isn't a laughing matter, Charles. It's my life, my future, and my career you're interfering with. If you can't see that then I really don't think we have a future together.' As she said those words he got some idea of the devastation he'd once wreaked on her. It felt as though someone had taken hold of his heart and squeezed it until the pain was so great he was sure he might die.

She'd been hesitant about starting over again here until she'd seen a commitment from him, telling her he would make a good father and he was no longer that man she'd believed had run out on her with no good reason. He'd thought he'd delivered with the prospect of employment at the hospital. Apparently not.

'I just wanted you to stay,' he muttered, feeling utterly pathetic that he'd failed her again.

'It's always about what *you* want, isn't it, Charles? You know I'd hoped we'd moved on from the past, but this proves we're no further on than we've ever been. Everything has to be on your terms, with no thought to how it affects me. You haven't changed at all, but I have. I'm no longer prepared to be that woman who'll wait until you get bored again.'

'Harriet, please, we can sort this out. I've messed up. Tell me what I can do to fix this.' He wasn't above begging if that's what it would take for her to give him another chance. This time he had much more to lose if she walked out of his life for good. He loved her more now than he ever had. Along with the baby he might never get to meet.

'If you'd changed from the man who ended our engagement without even talking to me about it, I wouldn't have to tell you what to do. We're only going to make each other miserable trying to force this relationship to work simply so you can have us where you want us. If it's okay with you, I'll spend the night and leave tomorrow. I have a few things to sort out and some goodbyes to say. We can work out access arrangements when the baby is born. In the circumstances you'll understand I want full custody. After all, I tried to do things your way.'

He sighed his reluctant acceptance. How could he object when she was right? If she loved him this wouldn't be so difficult, but he couldn't force her to feel the same way he did about her.

He should never have stepped out of his shoes as Laird and medical professional when he knew the heartache that caused from previous experience. Now he'd have to start the grieving process all over again. Grieving for the loss of the woman he loved, his child and the family he wasn't destined to have.

CHAPTER TEN

'I'M SORRY THINGS turned out this way.' Charles walked out the door as though he'd just cancelled a phone contract.

Harriet, on the other hand, had just had her whole world ripped out from under her. Again.

She managed to stay upright until he was out of the room, then her legs gave way and she collapsed onto the bed, too stunned to even cry. The moment she'd decided to seduce Charles in London she'd set herself up for a fall. If she hadn't given in to temptation she wouldn't have to go through this heartbreak for a second time.

Ending it with him was the last thing she wanted to do but she'd done so in self-defence. By making decisions for her without consulting her, it was clear he'd learned nothing. The relationship was never going to work. Especially once the baby was here and he started taking over there too. If he was incapable of changing, of considering her thoughts and feelings, she would end up the one getting hurt. There was a baby to think about in all of this too. The only option she could see now was to walk away and save what little there was left of her heart. It wasn't any easier to do second time around, even if it was through her choice this time.

She lay back on the bed and wondered when she'd started thinking of this place as home when it held so many panful memories for her. Now there was one more to add if she ever had the stupid idea of coming back. Whatever arrangements they made regarding the baby's upbringing, she couldn't put herself through this again.

Harriet curled up into a ball, her arm wrapped around her belly. It was only when she thought about their baby that the tears finally broke free and trickled from the corners of her eyes. It was just going to be the two of them from now on. Like her and her mum all over again. Except she'd make sure she had a job and a home to return to in case of this very eventuality.

Damn Charles Ross-Wylde for making her fall in love with him again. Now not only was she going to be a single mum, struggling to juggle motherhood and a career, but he'd damaged her heart beyond all repair this time. Along with her trust.

He'd offered her a job, a home and a place in his bed. The only thing he hadn't been able to give her was the love she so desperately wanted from him. Charles had waited until she'd fallen in love with the idea of being part of a family here with him, then snatched it away by repeating the same mistakes.

If she'd kept driving that first night and never come back, she'd be in a different head space than she was in now. A few days over Christmas feeling sorry for herself would've been nothing compared to this. She'd seen the possibilities of living at Heatherglen and becoming part of the family, but she would have to leave it all behind to look out for herself because no one else was going to do it for her.

* * *

'You're up early this morning. All that excitement with Harri must have kept you awake.'

Esme was refilling Dougal's water bowl when Charles made his way downstairs to the kitchen. Last night had left him drained but not in the way Esme probably imagined.

'Have you seen her?'

'Not yet. So, how do you really feel about the Dougal adoption plan?'

'The what?'

'Don't tell me you didn't get around to discussing it. Me and my big mouth.'

'No, we...er...had some other things going on.'

Esme stuck her fingers in her ears. 'Ugh. Stop. I don't want to hear what my brother and his girlfriend got up to last night.'

'Then tell me what it is you're wittering on about.'

She grabbed the two slices of toast as they popped up and began buttering them as though this was any ordinary morning and not the day after Charles had lost everything precious to him. 'Harriet had the bright idea that you two should adopt Dougal and keep him here at the castle.'

Charles stopped castigating his sister long enough to consider the implications of that news. 'Harriet wanted *us* to adopt Dougal?'

'Yes.' Esme munched on her breakfast, giving nothing else away about Harriet's secret pet project but it told Charles all he needed to know. Harriet *had* thought about staying on and making a life with him here. Taking on a dog was a commitment for the family they should have become. It was his blundering in, trying to secure her employment, that had messed everything up. If he'd left her to come to her own conclusion about what she wanted, instead of trying to force her hand, she wouldn't be leaving him.

He had been selfish. All this time he'd spent convincing her this was the place to raise the baby, he'd never once considered what would make her happy. He was asking her to give up everything she had achieved in London so he could have her and the baby here without disrupting his life. The truth was he didn't have a life worth living without Harriet in it.

He'd sent her away twelve years ago rather than make her fit into this world and now that's exactly what he was trying to do. She was the one expected to make all the concessions in this scenario he'd conjured up when it was clear it should've been him making the compromises to prove how much he loved her. He hoped it wasn't too late to do that.

With renewed determination to get their relationship on track he headed for the door. 'Esme, if Harriet comes through this way I need you to stall her.'

'What do you mean?'

'She wants to go back to London. I need you to keep her here until I get back, okay?'

'What is going on with you, Charles?' She was waving the remnants of her toast at him and if she knew how badly he'd screwed things up with Harriet, she'd be chucking it at him. He was going to do his best to fix things before Esme resorted to violence.

'I'm trying to get myself a life,' he answered, on his way out the door.

'Well, don't be long. We have a party to sort out.' Esme apparently had faith that he could do that in one afternoon. As Charles got into his car and set off for Glasgow, he prayed she was right. After all, he had everything to lose if he didn't get it right this time.

Harriet had intended to leave first thing, but she'd fallen fully clothed into an exhausted sleep so deep she hadn't heard her phone alarm go off. It had been the sound of a car door slamming outside that had finally woken her. Although she hadn't thought it possible, the sight of Charles driving away saddened her even more. If he wasn't even prepared to fight for her there really was no way back for them.

She took her time getting ready and packing up the last of her things. With Charles gone she didn't have the same urgency. Besides, she still had to say goodbye to Esme. Harriet was surprised to see her still sitting in the kitchen when she was usually at work by this time.

'Hi, Harriet. Can I get you anything to eat for breakfast?' Esme being nice to her was the last thing she needed. Much more of this and she'd start blubbing and tell her how much she loved her brother. She'd have to get out of here before she talked herself back into staying and condemned herself to a life with someone incapable of putting her first.

'No, thanks. I'm going to head back to London. I have a lot to sort out.'

She didn't enjoy keeping Esme in the dark, but she could do without any more drama. She was feeling too raw from the fallout to be exposed to someone else's pain. It was only fair someone considered Esme's feelings in these matters too, but she had to work through her own first.

'When?'

'Today. Now. As soon as I've woken up properly.' She wasn't looking forward to the long drive home, but she'd have to do it before she was faced with Charles again. There was no guarantee she'd maintain her dignity if that happened and her self-preservation was replaced with the overwhelming love for him she couldn't seem to bury.

'No! You can't!' Esme's outburst was so loud it send Dougal scampering back to his bed with his tail between his legs.

'I have to.'

'But—but it's—Hogmanay. We have our big Hogmanay party tonight. You can't miss that.'

'I'm really not in a partying mood.' It was one thing to pretend to Esme that nothing had happened to spoil her time here but putting on a brave face for a house full of strangers would require an inner strength she no longer possessed.

'It's wonderful, Harriet. Everyone comes together for the party. We have music and enough whisky that we can usually persuade Charles to sing.'

That did catch her interest. It reminded her of the night she'd met him at university. At one of those alcohol-fuelled affairs where it had been too noisy to even think straight. Then Charles had picked up a guitar, begun strumming and that velvety Scottish accent had captivated everyone in the room. It was a long time since she'd heard him sing. The memory of it did nothing to alleviate her pain.

'I'm sure I wouldn't be missed.'

'Oh, but you would. Hogmanay is a time for us all to be together. You haven't seen anything until you've been to our Hogmanay party.'

'I'm due back at work.' She knew the lame excuse wouldn't work but she attempted it anyway, her defences at an all-time low.

'There'll be dancing and fireworks and don't forget all the men in kilts.' Esme sensed her weakness and pounced. There was one man in particular who'd look delectable in the family tartan, but even the promise of that sight wasn't enough for Harriet to prolong her inevitable departure.

'Please, say you'll be there, Harriet. It's our way of saying goodbye to the past and welcoming in a new start.' The way Esme described it, celebrating Hogmanay at Heatherglen was tempting. The closure she needed before starting over as a mother to this baby who needed her to love it enough for both parents. She could always slip away during the fireworks…

'You can't leave anyway. The caterers have stuffed up. I'm going to need you to go shopping for me.' Esme pulled out a pad of paper from a drawer and started scribbling a list on it.

'What? No. Can't you get someone else to do it?' She'd end up with a serious case of trolley rage if forced to endure the hordes stocking up as though they were preparing for the apocalypse on top of everything else.

'There is no one else. I'm waiting for the fireworks guy to set up and Max is helping the band with their sound check. Charles delegated everything to me this year, and I can't have people turning up without food to offer them. I need your help.'

She was getting stressed if she was admitting she couldn't do this alone. If the event turned out to be a disaster Harriet knew she'd blame herself. Esme deserved someone to think of her for a change.

This was turning out to be the worst New Year's Eve in history.

Everywhere Harriet turned she was confronted with families stocking up with copious amounts of alcohol and snacks. Some were arguing over how much they actually needed, others looked bored to tears, but they were all preparing to see in the New Year together. At the stroke of midnight, she'd be getting ready to leave Heatherglen for the last time. Faced with the reality of ringing in the New Year alone made for a depressing picture.

She found herself wandering away from the grocery aisles towards the clothing department. To the baby section. The tiny outfits drew her like a moth to a flame. Her eyes misted as she fingered the soft fabric and thought about preparing for the new arrival on her own. Something she and Charles should be doing together.

Charles no more wanted to host a party than he wanted to go back to a house without Harriet. It was a tradition he usually enjoyed, unlike the recurring break-ups. This year he was prepared to let Esme take over. With any luck she'd throw herself so deeply into preparations he could excuse himself altogether. How could he celebrate the start of a new year when he'd finished this one on such a low? Loving Harriet wasn't something he'd get over as soon as the clock struck midnight. Unfortunately, he didn't have a fairy godmother who could wave her magic wand

and make him happy again, or make Harriet love him.

He hadn't seen her today, and he prayed his sister had been able to come up with a plan to keep her there for the few hours he'd been absent. It would be devastating if he didn't get to see her one last time and beg for her forgiveness.

Charles braced himself for the onslaught of Dougal love and whatever else waited for him behind Heatherglen's doors. If Esme was on her own and Harriet had gone, he'd never forgive himself and his sister would kill him once she found out how stupid he'd been. He could only hope with the upcoming party, the ear-blasting would be short-lived.

As predicted, as soon as he set foot inside the family home, Dougal was there to greet him. He reached down to stroke the only one who'd be pleased to see him, no matter what. When he glanced up from his crouched position on the floor he met those anguished eyes that had haunted him since last night.

'Esme wanted me to stay for the party.'

The sight of her when he thought he'd convinced himself he might never see her again hit him so hard it almost knocked him onto his backside.

'Can you give Harriet and me a minute, sis?' He was aware he was on borrowed time with Harriet now, especially if she worked out he'd been behind the ruse to get her to delay leaving for a while.

'I don't think there's any point—'

'Sure.' Thankfully, Esme cut off Harriet's protests and nipped out the door before she got dragged into the conversation.

'Can we talk?' He sat down at the table and pulled out a chair for Harriet. She remained standing.

'I don't think there's anything left to say, Charles.'

'I think there is. I hear you made plans for Dougal to become a permanent feature here?'

Harriet grabbed a cloth and began to clean down the work surfaces, which already looked spotless to Charles. 'It was just an idea I had. I'm sure Esme will find somewhere else for him.'

'You were going to make a decision like that without talking to me about it first?'

She spun around to face him. 'Rehoming a dog is not the same as transferring a person's job to a different country without telling her.'

'I know. I know. What I'm trying to say is that we were both doing things we thought would benefit each other. I wasn't trying to control your life, but I was guilty of not taking your feelings into consideration.'

'Why would you cut me out of decisions like that again after everything we've been through? You know how hard it's been for me to trust you again and then you go and do exactly the same thing.'

'I realise that. Probably too late, but I swear I will do whatever it takes for you to be happy from now on. All that matters to me is you and the baby.'

'I wish I could believe that.'

'Surely the fact you were willing for us to take on Dougal said you were thinking about staying on here? Deep down you must know how much I care about you or you'd never even have considered that sort of commitment.'

'It wasn't my feelings that were ever in

question. I love you, Charles. I've always loved you. Why else do you think this has been so hard?'

'Then what the hell are we doing to ourselves?' Hearing her say those words was all Charles needed to know he'd done the right thing in the end. He crossed the floor so he could be closer to her, wanting to take her in his arms, but she dodged around him and resumed her cleaning.

'I'm sorry but, ultimately, nothing else has changed. Except I called you out on your behaviour this time.'

'That's not true. A lot has changed. It just took the shock of potentially losing you to make me realise that. The clinic is up and running. They don't need me here any more. Esme could easily take over Heatherglen.'

'What are you saying, Charles?' Harriet stopped scrubbing invisible stains to stare at him. Knowing he was saying something she wanted to hear gave him the courage to carry on.

He pulled out a piece of paper and handed it to her. 'I went to see my solicitor this morning. This is simply a letter to confirm my intent, contracts are in the process of being written.'

She scanned the letter his solicitor had drawn up this morning under duress. He wasn't happy that Charles was willing to sign away his inheritance so easily, but this was a sacrifice he was only too willing to make if it meant he and Harriet could be together.

'I can't let you do this.' Harriet folded the letter and tucked it back into his jacket pocket. She was so close he could feel her warmth, smell her perfume, and he so desperately wanted to kiss her again. He wouldn't, though. Not unless he was sure he wanted him to.

'Oh? You're telling me what I can or can't do now?' He couldn't help but smirk at the irony in that. Really, he didn't mind when it showed she cared about him.

She gave him a sidelong look. 'This is different. Heatherglen is your life. I can't let you give that up.'

'You and the baby are my life now. I was asking too much of you, expecting you to give up your home, your job and everything else to move here. If you can still picture a future with me I'm fully prepared to follow you back to London. I'm sure I can find work there and we can come back and visit Esme anytime.' The answer had been staring him in the face all along. Harriet wanted him to make a commitment, a gesture big enough that she would stop fearing the worst. That he was going to leave her on her own again.

He'd fulfilled the promise he'd made to honour his brother and father and he'd seen Esme build a business and fall in love. Now it was time to focus on what was important to him. Harriet.

'This is all so...overwhelming.' Harriet wanted to believe she could have it all, but only a few hours ago she'd been getting ready to say goodbye for ever, convinced Charles didn't love her enough to change. Now he was offering to give up everything and go back to London with her. It was everything she wanted yet she was afraid of taking that final step with him again. Her head was spinning with the possibilities awaiting them but there was still something holding her back.

'I'll do whatever it takes to prove to you this family is all that I want. Say the word and I'll quit working altogether to be a stay-at-home dad. I just can't lose you again.'

She would never ask him to do any of the things he was willing to give up, but these weren't things he would say lightly. 'You'd do that for me?'

'I'd do that for us. For our family.' He stroked his thumb across her cheek and placed a ghost of a kiss on her lips. Enough for her to crave more. Except he let go of her again. 'I won't put you under any pressure to make a decision now. You need to do what's right for you.'

Sound advice. If only she knew what that was.

'Esme, this isn't the food I brought back from the supermarket.' Harriet saw the plates of haggis, neeps and tatties and home-made black bun, a rich fruit cake wrapped in pastry, and knew she'd been played.

'There was a bit of a mix-up. The caterers arrived not long after you left.' With the party in full swing, Esme had finally taken a break herself to get something to eat from the buffet laid out in the marquee.

'Uh-huh? You couldn't have phoned to let me know?'

Esme waved her away. 'I was busy. There's no harm done.'

As though Harriet wasn't suspicious enough about Esme's whole part in getting her to stay, she gave Charles a little wink before she disappeared with Max.

'Why do I get the feeling you had a rather large hand in the great catering mishap?' she asked Charles.

'I thought we needed more time to get our act together.' Charles slid his hands around Harriet's waist and kissed her neck.

'Well, one of us did.' She should've been angry that he'd concocted that supermarket trolley dash and wasted her afternoon, but it showed he had been fighting for them after all. While she'd been dispatched on a fool's errand, Charles had been signing his life away in a solicitor's office to prove his commitment to her. It was worth all the cloak and dagger shenanigans in the end when it made them both consider what was most important to them. Right now, she was content to be with Charles. The man who was willing to give up everything just to be with her.

He kissed her again. 'It's almost midnight and I promised I'd get up and sing. Although I'm not sure I've had nearly enough whisky yet to do that.'

'You have to. I've been looking forward to that all evening.' She turned around in his arms and fluttered her eyelashes. This Hogmanay party reminded her of that first night they'd met. Hearing Charles sing again would be the perfect way to end it.

'In that case, I wouldn't want to disappoint you. Now, are you sure Dougal's safely locked away?'

'Yes, and I left the radio on for him so he doesn't get lonely, just as you asked.'

'Thank you.' He dropped another kiss on her lips and went to join the band on the stage. Thankfully, the weather had improved over the course of the day. Although the ground was muddy, the crowd was able to move outside to watch the band. It had the atmosphere of being at a music festival. Especially when most of them were wearing wellington boots to enable them to move unhindered across the wet fields.

Charles looked so handsome up there, singing traditional Scottish folk songs, wearing his kilt and playing the guitar, Harriet had become his number one groupie. Especially when he locked eyes with her and made her feel as though she was the only person here and he was singing directly to her.

'This last song is dedicated to the woman I love. Harriet, this one's for you.' As Charles began singing the slow ballad that had made her fall in love with him in the first place, tears streamed down her face. It was only now she realised she'd been waiting for him to say those words before those last barriers around her heart fell away.

All too soon the song was over, but she'd make sure he kept that guitar and kilt handy. She wanted to see them both on a regular basis.

'Ten, nine, eight...'

The band began the countdown and

Charles jumped down off the stage so he could be with her at midnight.

'Seven, six, five, four…' She pulled him close so he was beside her to toast in the new year. Andy, the guy she'd met in the lounge, was standing nearby with Esme and Max and she waved over to him. He looked nervous and was leaning heavily on his crutches, waiting for the cacophony of cheers and fireworks as though he was going into battle.

'Three, two, one.'

The place erupted as the sky lit up with explosions of colour and the crowd burst into a chorus of Auld Lang Syne, linking arms as they did.

'Are you doing okay, Andy?' She moved closer to where she could keep a closer eye on him even though he had people on either side to make sure this wasn't too much for him.

'You know what? I really am. I'm not in Afghanistan any more. Not even in my head. Happy New Year, Harriet. I think this is going to be the best one yet,' he said as he raised his glass of whisky.

'I think so too,' she said, and couldn't resist giving him a hug. It was so heart-warming to see another patient start anew after their recovery, whether from mental or physical impairment. As he joined Esme in letting off the party poppers and covering everyone around them in glitter and string, his laughter confirmed he'd passed his test and finally conquered his demons.

Charles grabbed her by the hand and pulled her towards the house.

'Where are we going? We're going to miss the party.' She looked back with longing at the throng of happy people celebrating with-out them.

'We can't miss the first footer,' He said as though she knew what he was talking about. Her expression must've given her away as he was compelled to explain.

'The first person to step into the house in the New Year.'

'Oh,' she said, still clueless as to why this was significant.

Sure enough they'd just made it inside be-fore someone knocked. Charles opened the door to a tall, black haired man and welcomed him in with a, 'Happy New Year.'

The dark stranger presented Charles with an array of gifts. 'Whisky, to drink and celebrate the New Year. Coal, so that your house will be warm, bring comfort and be safe for the year ahead. Shortbread, to make sure those in the household won't go hungry and a silver coin to bring prosperity.'

'Thank you. Now go on out back and get something for yourself to eat and drink.' Charles accepted the basket of gifts with one hand and clapped him on the back with the other, ushering him towards the party outside.

Once the mysterious visitor had gone, Charles opened the whisky and poured them two glasses. 'Happy New Year.'

Harriet clinked her glass to Charles's. 'Here's to the New Year, and our new life.'

'I'm so happy you're here to share this with me. There's only one thing that could make the moment more perfect, Harriet. That's why I wanted us to greet the first footer and bless us with good luck for the forthcoming year. Harriet Bell, will you marry me?'

'Yes. A thousand times, yes.' She threw her arms around his neck, uncaring about the whisky spilling everywhere. This was the ultimate commitment and there was nothing she wanted more than to marry this man and have his baby. As long she was with Charles she didn't care where they started their new life.

The truth had finally set them free, enabling them to raise their family in the best possible place. A home filled with love.

EPILOGUE

'DO YOU THINK we should call off the Christmas party?' Charles was doing lengths of the living room with the baby over his shoulder, trying to settle him.

'Thomas is just teething. He'll be fine.' Harriet was more enamoured than ever with her gorgeous husband now he was as attentive to their son as he was to her. They were enjoying their time off together over the festive period, even if sleep had become a thing of the past recently.

'It's not just for Thomas's benefit. I think it would be nice for us to have a quiet evening together.' Once their son had stopped crying, Charles was able to lay him down on the activity quilt he'd received from Auntie Esme for Christmas. The baby's attention now on the bright-coloured jungle animals on the fabric and the noisy attachments, his exhausted father collapsed onto the sofa beside his wife. He still had enough energy to give her a passionate kiss. Thankfully, parenthood hadn't diminished that side of their relationship.

'That does sound like heaven.' Chilling out by the fire, spending quality time together, was more appealing than the idea of rushing around making sure their guests had enough to eat or drink all evening.

'Surely we could skip it for one year?'

'I don't think people would mind. Aksel and Flora are probably comfortable enough where they are without having to trail out here from the village in the cold. The same could be said for Lyle and Cassandra, even though they don't have as far to travel.'

At this time of year most people were content to stay with the ones they loved. The difference for Harriet this year was that she had people to stay at home with.

'What about Esme?' Charles gave her the face that said their plans for a quiet night had just been thwarted.

'You know she'll want to see her nephew

and having Max and Esme isn't the same as hosting a party. We can still have a quiet night in.'

'You think? Just wait until she has us playing musical chairs and hide and seek.' Although he was denying it, Harriet knew Esme's excitement was part of the tradition around here.

'As long as I don't have to start cooking, or even get dressed, I don't care. I'm going to slob out today.'

'Me too.' Charles stretched out along the settee and put his feet up. They were both overdue a good rest after the year they'd had getting her transferred from London and making plans for the research centre. Not to mention their wedding in the middle of it all. Now, with Aksel building an adventure centre on the estate, the year ahead was going to be another busy one for Heatherglen. She would never have expected Charles to give up Heatherglen when it had become a family home for all of them.

They heard paper rustling in the corner and Charles lifted his head. 'Dougal! He's in the presents again.'

Harriet watched with amusement as the two did battle over the new scarf Joanie had knitted Charles for Christmas. She couldn't seem to do enough to thank them both for saving her life.

'Give me that back, you daft mutt.' Charles was growling almost as much as Dougal, who thought he was being treated to a new game, and Thomas was gigging at the spectacle too.

Yes, this was her crazy family, and she wouldn't trade it for anything.

* * * * *

Welcome to the
Pups that Make Miracles quartet!

Highland Doc's Christmas Rescue
by Susan Carlisle

Festive Fling with the Single Dad
by Annie Claydon

Making Christmas Special Again
by Annie O'Neil

Their One-Night Christmas Gift
by Karin Baine

All available now!